THE GODLING CLUB

STEPHEN PENNER

ISBN-13: 978-0-6155828-4-9
ISBN-10: 0-6155828-4-2

The Godling Club

This is a work of fiction. Any similarity with real persons or events is purely coincidental. Persons, events, and locations are either the product of the author's imagination, or used fictitiously.

Cover image by Kriss Szkurlatowski. Used with permission.
Cover design by Stephen Penner.

THE
GODLING
CLUB

ONE1

When you turn fourteen, one birthday party just isn't enough. Although, really, the only party I cared about was the middle one. The one Chelsea Winters was coming to.

I'd finally worked my way into her clique of the most popular girls at school. What better way to celebrate my birthday than finally being one of the cool kids? Chelsea and her entourage were coming at 2:00, to say, 'Happy birthday, Jeni Tanaka. Welcome to the club.'

Of course, my mom didn't get how important it was, how hard it was to get there, how much I'd given up to make it happen. She started telling me stories about when she was my age, and hunting dinosaurs with spears, uphill in the snow, back when people still used paper money and listened to music on 'stereos'— whatever those were.

So she made me invite my old friends too. Especially Kyle. He'd been my best friend since first grade. NOT my boyfriend. I didn't have a boyfriend, but if I did, it would *not* have been Kyle Emerson. He was super nice, but not exactly cool. In fact, he was exactly not cool.

The first thing Chelsea asked when I invited her was, "That Kyle kid's not coming, is he?"

"That loser?" I made myself laugh. "No way."

"Good." Chelsea's voice was like ice.

But when I told Mom I wasn't inviting Kyle, she went all parent on me—droning on and on about true friendship, and youthful folly, and biggest regrets—and said I had to invite him. So I did.

To the 3:00 party.

Mom didn't say I had to tell him the truth.

I knew Chelsea and her friends would never stay for a whole hour. They were making an appearance, but they had other appearances to make. So Chelsea would be long gone from the second party by the time Kyle showed up for the third party.

But the very first party would be at 1:30. The *family* party. Mom had insisted. The usual stuff about family and blood being thicker than water and all the stuff she usually said when she was overcompensating for Dad divorcing her and moving to California with his secretary. But then she went all stealth ninja on me and told me she'd explain at 1:30, then I'd understand why she'd have to pull me aside and give me my gift right at 2:12, the exact moment, Seattle-time, I was born. The exact moment I turned fourteen.

Whatever.

I wasn't really looking forward to a present that required a preparatory lecture, but she wouldn't take no for an answer.

Which is why, looking back, I should have realized how strange it was that she got a text at 1:15, then suddenly announced she had to run to the store for one more thing. And why I should have paid more attention to that black BMW parked down the street that followed after her. I figured it was just Chelsea checking out my house to see if she was willing to be photographed there.

Boy, was I wrong.

1:30 came and went and Mom wasn't back yet. At first I didn't even notice, then I was glad. I had a lot of prep work still for Chelsea's arrival. The last thing I wanted to do was sit down and listen to her tell me how much she loved me, how proud she was of me turning into a young woman (Awkward! Next subject please), and 'Here's the cameo brooch'—or whatever—'your great, great, great grandmother gave me when *I* turned fourteen.'

Cameos were so in. They looked great with nose studs.

So when 2:00 finally came, I wasn't even thinking about Mom. I was sitting in the living room, trying not to peer out the window every three seconds. It was finally going to happen. After fourteen horrible years as the ugly kid, the dumb kid, the weird kid—finally, I was going to be the cool kid. Or at least the cool kid's friend. Well, one of her friends.

Hey, I had to start somewhere.

Of course, Chelsea was fashionably late. 2:06 by the living room clock. 2:05 would have been too obvious.

"Hey, Chelsea." I tried to sound cool as I opened the door.

"Hey, Jeni." She stepped in and immediately appraised my home. Then she smiled. "Nice house."

Oh yeah, I was in. Goodbye, Loserville. Hello, Cooltown.

That exchange had taken about a minute. I had five minutes left of being cool.

It was a sunny May afternoon. I led everyone through the newly remodeled kitchen (Mom was going to do it anyway eventually, so I begged her to finish before my birthday) and out onto the new deck. She'd insisted on the artificial plastic wood junk because, she said, it was 'easier to maintain.' Whatever. I just prayed Chelsea wouldn't notice.

Drinks were out and music was playing in the background.

It had taken some major intelligence to find out Chelsea's favorite thing to drink was lemonade with a lime slice in it and her favorite type of music was German techno-pop—not that British trash.

Chelsea sat down with her lemonade and surveyed my backyard. Then she nodded approvingly.

"Tanaka, you're all right. Me and the girls want you to hang out with us." She paused. "Besides, we need another brunette."

Everyone laughed. Of course they did: it was Chelsea's joke. It was a lame joke, but I laughed too. Hey, this was important.

"So what do you say, Tanaka?" Chelsea raised her glass to me. "You wanna hang with the cool girls?"

What did I say? What did I say?!

Well, as it turns out, I said nothing.

I opened my mouth to answer—to shout 'Yes!' at the top of my lungs—but I couldn't speak. In fact, I couldn't move at all. I could barely see.

I just stared at Chelsea, my jaw hanging open. Then I tipped forward onto my face, right on top of the plastic deck.

"Tanaka?" I heard Chelsea say, but her voice was as distant as a church bell.

I think I started convulsing. My insides felt like they were melting and freezing at the same time. Everything looked golden and silver. It seemed like I could hear for a hundred miles.

"Oh my God, she's spazzing out."

"Let's get out of here!"

"Should we help her?"

"No way. She's a freak. Let's go!"

They left me alone there, flailing, convulsing, moaning, drooling. All alone.

And yet I wasn't alone.

Whatever was happening to me, it was alive and it wanted

me. Wanted to get inside me, to become a part of me, to take me over.

I forgot all about Chelsea and the Gang, and focused on whatever was attacking me. I knew my life depended on it. Something was invading me and I had to repel it.

"Get... out," I managed to growl as I pushed myself up onto my hands and knees. "This... this is *my* body. Get *out!*"

I could feel the invader's thoughts, or at least its emotions. It was surprised by my resistance. 'Stunned' might be a better a word. Then it was confused. Then sad.

And then it was gone.

I collapsed and passed out.

When I woke up, I was flat on my back on that stupid plastic deck. I'd drooled all over myself, blood was drying in my ears, and I'd peed my brand new, two-hundred-dollar jeans.

Kyle was kneeling over me. "Oh my God, Jeni. What the heck happened to you?"

TWO2

Ugh.

Kyle was so uncool he still said 'heck' instead of 'hell.'

I was so glad to see him.

"Nnnhghnnh," was all I could manage to say. I tried to sit up, but my muscles wouldn't respond. It was probably just as well. The very thought of moving made we want to throw up.

"Happy birthday," he deadpanned. "Looks like I missed the party."

He looked over at the drink table. "You're not drunk, are you?"

"No, I'm not drunk," I groaned. I tried again to sit up and managed to prop myself up into a painful little ball. I rested my throbbing head in my hands. "And yes, you missed the party."

He didn't say anything for a few seconds. Probably trying to figure out how the party could be over already.

"Did you know you peed your pants?" he finally asked.

I looked up at him through my fingers. "Thanks." I hung my head back down and held an open hand out to him. "Can I get a lemonade, please?"

"Sure thing." He hopped over to the table and unscrewed the cap of a lemonade bottle. "You want a lime slice in it?"

I glared at him again between my fingers. "No. I hate limes."

He handed me the lemonade bottle and sat down on the deck next to me.

"Ooh, is this Plast-O-Deck?" He rubbed the smooth planks. "Nice."

I just put the cool bottle against my forehead and tried not to puke.

"So what happened?" he tried again.

I took a deep breath. "I'm not really sure," I admitted. "I'm not even sure where to begin."

"Begin at the beginning," Kyle grinned, and he took a sip of his own lemonade.

I nodded. "Okay, okay." I wiped the bottle against my forehead, then took the tiniest sip. My mouth was parched but my stomach was still queasy. A single sip was the best compromise. "Chelsea got here at two-oh-six—"

That was as far as I got.

"Chelsea?" Kyle screeched. "Chelsea *Winters*? That, that, that... witch?"

It was usually cute how Kyle didn't swear. Right then it was irritating. Although, really, I was irritated at myself that I forgot I'd lied to him.

"You invited Chelsea Winters to your birthday party?" Kyle was indignant. "She calls me names at school—if she even talks to me at all. She's so mean! Why would you invite her?"

I didn't answer. Instead I kept my eyes closed while I waited for him to figure the rest of it out.

It didn't take long. "Wait a minute. Two-o-six? The party was at two, not three?"

"I'm sorry, Kyle," I managed to croak. "It's kinda hard to explain."

"I wish it were," Kyle muttered. He took another drink of his lemonade, then started to get up. "Maybe I should just get going."

"No, Kyle, don't leave!" I reached out and grabbed his arm. The sudden movement sent my head, and my stomach, spinning again. "Please. Don't leave. That's what Chelsea and her friends did when it happened."

Kyle sat back down. "When what happened, Jeni?"

"I— I'm not sure, Kyle," I answered. "I can't really explain it. I don't know what happened."

"*I* know," came a deep voice from behind us.

We both whirled around—ouch, my head—and saw a strange boy standing in my backyard, right at the edge of the deck. He was a year—maybe two—older than us, with thick black hair and a sharp, strong nose.

He jumped onto the deck. "And I will explain."

THREE3

"I will explain," the strange boy repeated, "but on the way. There's no time to lose."

"Wait just a second." Kyle tried to sound brave. I could hear how his voice got a little higher and nasally when he was nervous. "Who are you?"

"My name is Tommy," he answered. "Tommy Bluehorse. I am the godling for Awonawilona."

I looked up at him, then at Kyle. Kyle looked back at me and we both shrugged.

"What's a godling?" I asked.

"Who's I-wanna-uh-lo-uh, whatever you said?" Kyle added.

"I will explain everything," Tommy repeated, "but we must get going. We don't have much time. You may have ruined everything."

I was stunned. "Me? I didn't do anything."

"You peed your pants," Kyle reminded me.

"Oh nice." I gestured toward Tommy Bluehorse, Godling to Awonawilona. "We have company."

I finally felt well enough to stand, so I got up—slowly—and

faced our guest. He looked taller from down on the Plast-O-Deck. "What do you mean I ruined everything?"

Instead of answering he took a firm hold of my arm and said, "Change your clothes. Then we will leave."

I didn't like being grabbed. Kyle liked it even less.

"Let go of her!" he commanded. I was impressed for a second, until he started his capoeira moves.

Kyle couldn't take tae kwon do like the rest of the kids. Instead he studied capoeira, a Brazilian martial art that combined combat with dance. So he was bobbing and sliding back and forth, like a crab about to stand on its head.

I thought Tommy would start laughing, like all the kids at school did, but instead he let go of my arm and took a respectful step back. "I meant no disrespect. I'm just eager to get going."

Kyle stopped his bobbing and weaving. He wasn't sure what to do. Even though he had worked his way up to a blue belt, no one was impressed by a martial art you had to convince people even existed.

I stepped in. "Let's all just calm down. Give me five minutes to clean up and clear my head, then I'll be back down."

"Then we can leave," Tommy said.

"Then we can *talk*," I countered.

I looked at Kyle, but he was still jacked up from his Brazilian karate intimidation victory. He looked back at me and raised a fist. "Yo."

I rolled my eyes and went inside. Ten minutes later I was showered, dressed, and back outside. But not on the deck. They had walked around front to where Tommy had parked his used hatchback. Tommy was leaning against the car. Kyle was standing on the curb, talking about something that was obviously boring Awonawilona's godling.

"You said five minutes," Tommy complained as soon as I walked up.

"I lied." I answered. "Anyway, you said I ruined everything, so we're both exaggerating."

"I'm not exaggerating," Tommy asked. "You may well have set into motion a series of events which could destroy the entire world."

It sounded ridiculous, but part of me believed him. I didn't know what he was talking about, but I believed him. "Well, that sucks."

"You're having a pretty crappy birthday," Kyle observed.

I ignored him.

"So how did I ruin everything?" I asked Tommy.

He took a hold of my arm again, but in urgency, not anger. "You are the godling to Izamani no Mikoto. Or at least you were supposed to be. But you rejected her and now the entire world may be destroyed."

"Izamani no muh—?" I tried to say. "What's that?"

Tommy shoved his hands through his thick black hair. "There really is no more time for this. We must leave and we must leave now. It may already be too late."

I looked at Kyle, but all he did was shrug. I decided this was just too weird. I didn't even know this kid.

He opened his car door. "Come on, let's go."

I crossed my arms. "Sorry, Tommy Bluehorse. I'm gonna go back inside and wait for my mom to come home. And there's not a damn thing that can keep me from doing that."

So of course, that's when my house blew up.

FOUR4

The explosion threw all of us to the ground. When I finally managed to push myself to my hands and knees, I saw what was left of my home in flames.

"Now do you believe me?" Tommy asked. "Your mother has been kidnapped. We have to get to Japan to rescue her."

"Kidnapped?" I shrieked, even as the distant sound of sirens began to fill the air.

"Japan?" asked Kyle. "I've always wanted to go to Japan."

I grabbed him by the shirt and pressed my forehead against his. "Mom. Kidnapped. Focus."

"Right," squeaked Kyle. "Got it."

I let go and turned to Tommy. "What makes you think my mom was kidnapped?"

"You are a godling as well," Tommy ignored the question about my mother. "Or at least, you were supposed to be. But you rejected your spirit. Now Izamani no Mikoto is lost and we enter unknown—and dangerous—territory."

"You keep saying I'm a godling," I bit off on the change of topic for a moment. "What's a godling?"

"Long ago," Tommy explained, "people recognized that spirits of creation and destruction—of good and evil, of right and wrong—permeated the Earth. Many of these ancient beliefs faded but the spirits live on. Today there are twelve pairs of creation and destruction spirits, from twelve of Earth's most ancient cultures. These spirits must reside inside a human host—a godling. I am the godling to Awonawilona, the Zuni spirit of creation. You were supposed to be the godling to Izamani no Mikoto, the Japanese spirit of creation."

"Why me?" I asked.

"Because you turned fourteen today," Tommy answered. "The spirit passes from parent to child upon the child's fourteenth birthday."

"Wasn't your grandma from Japan?" Kyle asked.

"Thanks, Sherlock," I hissed at him. "I get the connection."

Tommy leaned back and stared at me through narrowed eyes. "Your mother didn't tell you, did she?"

"My mother?" I answered. "A godling? She's never said anything about being a godling. She can barely cook dinner without burning it. I don't think she's a reincarnated goddess."

Tommy Bluehorse shook his head. "It's not reincarnation. The spirit is immortal. We simply offer it a temporary home."

Kyle looked at me. I looked back and shrugged. What Tommy was claiming was unreal. On the other hand, whatever had happened to me was very real. And what I felt then matched what he was saying now.

Tommy was resting his chin on his fist, deep in thought. Finally he looked at me again. "What was the last thing your mother said to you?"

I thought for a moment. "She got a text message and said she had to run the store for one last thing. She never came back."

"What was the text message?" Kyle asked.

I shook my head. "She didn't tell me."

"Did you notice anything else?" Tommy asked. "Did anyone follow her?"

My heart sank. "Oh my God, a car followed her! I thought it was Chelsea, but it wasn't. A car, a black car followed her as she drove away."

Tommy offered a knowing nod.

"Nakajima."

"Where's Nakajima?" I asked.

"Nakajima's not a where, he's a who." Tommy opened his car door. "Get in. I'll explain on our way to the airport."

FIVE5

"Hiroshi Nakajima," Tommy explained as he drove. "The godling to Shinigami, the Japanese spirit of destruction. He must have known today was your birthday."

"So what?" I asked from the front passenger seat.

"So he knew you wouldn't accept Izamani no Mikoto if you didn't understand what was going on," Tommy said. "He prevented your mom from telling you in time. Now a creation spirit is hostless and the spirits of destruction have the upper hand."

I was starting to get mad that nobody had told me anything but now I was being blamed for unleashing the forces of evil upon the world.

"Why did the spirit have to leave Jeni's mom in the first place?" Kyle asked from the backseat.

"The spirits need youthful godlings to thrive," Tommy explained. "At least the creation spirits do. So whenever a creation godling's eldest child turns fourteen, the spirit transfers to the child. There's a ceremony, but it is never revealed until just before the transfer."

"So is Nakajima a teenager too?" I asked.

Tommy smiled ruefully. "No, Nakajima is a very rich Japanese man in his fifties. The destruction godlings are usually selfish people. They avoid having children so they can keep the spirit forever. It is only when they die that the spirit is released. It then combs the Earth for a new godling. Nakajima is getting older. This must be part of a plan to hold onto his power."

"So what do we do now?" Kyle asked.

'We'? I thought. This wasn't his problem. But I didn't say anything.

"We have to find the spirit," Tommy said.

"No," I replied. "We have to find my mom."

Before Tommy and I could start arguing, Kyle stepped in. "I bet if we find one, we'll find the other."

I wasn't so sure, but Tommy smiled. "Agreed."

Then he handed me his smartphone. "We need to contact the others."

I took the phone. "Others?"

"The other godlings," Tommy said. "Look for the Glitter app on the home screen."

"Glitter?"

"It's our social network site."

I looked down at the phone. Right there at the top was an icon of a little blue Pegasus. "How many of you are there?"

"Twelve," Tommy answered instinctively. Then he corrected himself. "Eleven now, I guess."

"And you need a social networking site?" I questioned.

"Not everybody uses it," Tommy replied. "Mostly the younger ones. But it's a good place to connect."

I clicked the icon and the screen filled with Tommy's post stream. His most recent was at 3:09. 'Something wrong at Tanaka house. No word from @Izamani_no_Mikoto. Will check it out.

#transferfail.'

"Does my mom have an account?" I wasn't sure I wanted to see it.

"Uh, no," Tommy stammered. "Not really. She was kinda the oldest of us. Not really into the whole social media thing."

I was kind of relieved. This whole your-mom-was-a-goddess-but-now-she's-been-kidnapped thing was freaking me out enough. I didn't need to read her posts. '#amgoddessing.'

"So who's the oldest now?" I decided to turn the conversation. "You?"

Tommy smiled. "No, not me. But that's who I want you to call. Find the profile for Ling and click on his phone number."

"Ling?" I confirmed while navigating through the screens. There it was. Ling Tau Meng. Right after Cathy Tanaka. I was way tempted to click on my mom's profile, but I wasn't ready for that yet. Weird that my mom's contact info was in the phone of some teenage Native American godling. I shook my head a little to clear it, then clicked on Ling Tau's name. His email and phone popped up and I clicked on the phone number, then handed the phone to Tommy.

As I did so, I looked back at Kyle and raised my eyebrows. He just shrugged in reply. It was exactly how I felt too.

Tommy started talking into the phone. "*Ta yu wo.*"

"Is that Chinese?" Kyle whispered to me.

I stared at him for a second. "No, it's Canadian."

Kyle nodded. "Oh."

Then he sneered at me, realizing what I'd said. He was about to say something back so I hushed him so Tommy could hear.

"*Wo-men qu jichang.*"

Finally Tommy hung up and handed me the phone back.

"Wrong number?" I joked.

Tommy smiled, but only a little. "We're here," he announced.

I looked out the window and saw that we were driving into Seattle-Tacoma International Airport.

"What did Ling say?" I asked.

Tommy frowned. "He said he'd meet us in Tokyo. He's in Shanghai right now, but he has some matters to attend to, so it will take him longer to get there."

"What's he doing in Shanghai?" Kyle asked.

"He lives there," Tommy answered. "He's the godling to Pan Gu, the Chinese creation god. I told him what happened. Now that Izamani no Mikoto has left Jeni's mother, Ling is the oldest among us."

"How long will it take him to get to Tokyo?" I asked as Tommy pulled into a parking space in the airport's garage.

"He'll be about twelve hours behind us."

"Well," I tried to sound upbeat, "that gives us half a day to find my mom before he arrives."

We all piled out of the car, but Tommy was shaking his head as we walked toward the gates. "No, Ling doesn't think we should confront Nakajima alone. He told us to wait for him."

I considered sitting on my hands for twelve hours instead of trying to rescue my mom.

"Yeah," I said as we reached the ticketing windows. "That's not gonna work."

SIX6

"I know how you feel," Tommy started, but I cut him off.

"I don't think you do." I wasn't yelling, but I wasn't quiet either. "My mother has been kidnapped and I'm not going to sit around and wait for some guy I don't even know to finish his 'to do' list."

"Yeah," Kyle added. "What she said."

Tommy looked at Kyle for a long second, then back to me. "Before you condemn my suggestions, try to remember that the only reason you know that your mother was kidnapped, and by whom, and to where, is because of me."

He had a point.

"Three round trip tickets to Tokyo, please," Tommy told the saleslady.

She raised an eyebrow at the teenagers traveling alone, but then just said, "Passports and IDs, please."

"My passport was in my house," I whispered to Tommy.

"I don't even have a passport," whispered Kyle.

Tommy just smiled and handed the sales lady a credit card and three U.S. passports.

"The boy scouts aren't the only ones who are always prepared," he whispered back.

After a few minutes of furious keystrokes, the ticket lady slid our tickets, boarding passes, and even our alleged passports to us back across the counter. I was dying to see mine.

"Your flight leaves from gate 37," she said, before adding suspiciously, "No bags?"

"We're meeting family there," I explained.

Tommy gave me a surprised but approving smile.

We thanked the saleslady, took our paperwork and headed for the gate.

The pass through security was humiliating, but uneventful. I was glad I had taken the time to shower and change. But as I was putting my shoes and belt back on, Tommy suddenly grabbed my arm.

"Come with me!" he whispered and yanked me from my chair. I only had one shoe on and my belt was still in my hand.

Kyle didn't have either shoe on and his belt was hanging down from the one loop he'd managed to get it through. "What's going on?"

"Hush!" rasped Tommy. "Come on. Now."

He yanked me away from security and I followed him in an awkward hop as I tried to get my second shoe on. Kyle picked up his shoes and ran after us with his belt swinging and clanking against his leg.

Tommy pulled us through some doors marked 'Authorized Access Only.' Kyle and I finished getting dressed while Tommy peeked back into the terminal through the door crack.

"What's going on?" I whispered.

"Miguel Zapata," Tommy said. "That's what."

"That's 'who' would be better," Kyle whispered. He

shrugged at me. "Just sayin'."

Tommy turned back to glare at Kyle for a second, then went back to peering out into the airport.

"Who's Miguel Zapata?" I asked.

"Godling to Itzcoliuhqui," Tommy practically gasped. "Aztec god of destruction." Then, to himself, "How did he find us so fast?"

"What's he doing?" I asked as I finished fastening my belt.

"Walking toward Gate 37," Tommy answered. "This is bad. This is very bad."

He stood up and looked at the ceiling, pushing his hands through his thick, black hair. He moved away from the door so I took the opportunity to peek out. Across the way I could see a teenage boy, probably seventeen or eighteen, wearing a stylish outfit and sporting a tight, male model haircut.

"Ooh, he's cute," I said to myself. Unfortunately Kyle heard too. He wasn't my boyfriend, but there was still some tension there, so when he heard me, he said, way too loudly, "Oh, come *on*, Jeni!"

Miguel Zapata stopped dead in his tracks and began scanning the area. He looked right past our door, then back again.

"Oh good job, Kyle," I whisper-yelled. "I think he heard you."

"Let me see," Tommy pushed in and took my spot at the door.

"What were you thinking?" I continued to chastise Kyle in whispers.

"What were *you* thinking?" Kyle shot back. "You think the Aztec god of death is cute?"

"It's the Aztec god of destruction, not death," I pointed out. "And he's not the actual god, he's the godling."

"Well, I think he's gone too," Tommy whispered, still peering out the crack. "I don't see him anymore."

Just then the door swung open and Miguel Zapata smiled down at the crouching Tommy Bluehorse.

"*Hola,* Thomas."

"Run!" yelled Kyle but I was already halfway down the hall.

SEVEN7

The hallway turned sharp left then continued along a row of doors marked with numbers that meant nothing to me but probably made all sorts of sense to the airport employees. I could hear footsteps behind me so I ducked into the next door I came to, marked 47-K03.

It was some kind of baggage room. There were suitcases and crates and boxes all over the place, making narrow walkways between teetering towers of luggage. I zigzagged toward the back of the room just as I heard the door open and shut again. I dropped to the floor and held my breath.

I wasn't sure at first if someone had come in, or maybe had just looked inside and kept going down the hall.

It was silent for several seconds. I thought maybe I'd gotten lucky.

Then whoever it was bumped into a stack of suitcases and sent the top one tumbling onto the ground with a thump and the sound of something valuable inside breaking.

My heart was racing. I couldn't hold my breath anymore. I had to force myself not to pant even though I'd just sprinted down the hall.

I wanted to call out 'Hello?' in case it was Tommy or Kyle. But I didn't dare, in case it was Miguel.

I looked around to see if there was maybe a back door to the room, but it was impossible to see around the stacks of boxes and bags.

I got down on my hands and knees and started crawling toward the end of the row I found myself in. I was hoping to peek around the corner to get a glimpse of who was there or, better yet, to spy an exit. One hand, one knee at a time, I inched down the walkway to the end of the baggage towers. I didn't make so much as a squeak with my palm on the linoleum floor. But my efforts were in vain.

As I peered around the corner, my face inches from the floor, I got a close up view of a fashionable pair of men's leather shoes.

"*Hola*, Jeni Tanaka." Miguel's smile was as cold as when he'd opened that 'Authorized Access Only' door. And he was even cuter up close.

He reached out for me and I screamed, instinctively jumping up and pushing a stack of suitcases onto him. They didn't bury him in luggage by any means, but they knocked him off balance and that gave me enough time to jump to my feet and run out the back door I finally spotted from my standing position.

My ears filled with the roar of airplane engines. I was out on the tarmac.

And a baggage tractor was speeding right at me.

EIGHT8

This time it was the tractor driver who screamed. I was frozen to the spot, but he jerked the wheel hard to one side to avoid me. He missed me—thankfully—but he crashed into the wall of the airport, toppling the trailer and sending up a shower of suitcases. The tractor itself crumpled against the cement wall, crippling the machine. The driver was okay, but that car wasn't moving an inch without a tow truck, or maybe two.

That was great news for me, because it was blocking the door to room 47-K03. Miguel could only open it a few inches, banging it against the disabled tractor. It was wide enough that I could see him looking out, yelling something in Spanish. And it was wide enough that he could see me running away.

I was right outside the terminal, where all the huge planes parked to let passengers on and off through those portable sky bridges. I felt like an ant, scurrying beneath winged giants, not sure which way to turn to avoid getting squished. I needed to get back inside, so I could find Kyle and Tommy, so we could find Gate 37, so we could find my mom.

Then I heard someone yelling my name over the rush of

airplane noise.

"Jeni! Jeni!"

I swung my head around as I was running and spotted Kyle and Tommy running out onto the tarmac from a door farther down the hallway. That was good news and bad news. The good news was that I'd found Tommy and Kyle again. The bad news was that Miguel would be able to get out on the tarmac the same way. It wouldn't take him long to realize he wasn't going to move that luggage car by shoving on the door, and to make his way down the hall to the next available exit.

Tommy, Kyle, and I ran toward each other and met between two jetliners.

"How did you get out here?" Kyle yelled.

"Where's Miguel?" Tommy shouted.

"Never mind all that!" I screamed. "We have to find Gate 37!"

"No!" answered Tommy. "Miguel knows where were going. It's too dangerous."

"Not finding my mom is what's too dangerous!" I replied. "Besides, maybe he'll think we abandoned our plans—just like you want us to."

"Or maybe he'll find us out here!" Kyle shrieked, pointing back at the terminal.

Sure enough, Miguel had stepped through a door further down the hallway and was scanning the tarmac for us. It only took a moment. We were pretty obvious. When he saw us he smiled. Then he started walking toward us. Not even running. Too cocky.

I looked around and spotted a plane that was still connected to the terminal by its accordion walkway. More importantly, the ground crew was just lining up the little car to push the walkway away from the plane. But most importantly, the walkway connected to the terminal right below a pair of huge numbers: '37.'

"Come on!" I grabbed Tommy and Kyle's wrists and started sprinting toward the walkway.

We ran right past the surprised ground crew and up the attached staircase to the top of the walkway—and the entrance to the plane. As we reached the top I turned around and saw Miguel. He was finally running, but by the time he reached the steps, the three men in the ground crew had gotten out of their vehicle and blocked the walkway.

They weren't going to let anybody else up that ramp. And they were too busy with him to chase us. We ducked onto the walkway to the astonishment of the stewardess who was about to pull the plane door shut.

"Sorry we're late!" I shouted.

"Thanks for holding the plane!" added Kyle.

"We gave our boarding passes to the ground crew," lied Tommy.

The stewardess just stood there, so we slipped past her and onto the plane. Then she shook her head, pulled the door shut and locked it tight.

I exhaled loudly and patted Kyle on the back. "We did it!"

"Next stop Tokyo," he smiled.

The three of us headed into the passenger compartment to see if there we're even any seats available for us. As it turned out there were two together in the second to last row—right next to the bathroom, of course—plus another one a few rows up and on the other side of the plane. Kyle and I took the ones by the bathroom and Tommy sat in the other one.

The entire time the plane was pulling away from the terminal, I was just waiting for the abrupt stop followed by the announcement that we had to go back to the gate because of the unauthorized passengers. But the plane continued to pull away from the gate, then pivot and head forward to the runway. The only announcement came as we arrived at our place in the takeoff queue.

"Hello, everyone. This is your pilot speaking. I'd like to thank you all for you patience this morning as we fixed that minor mechanical problem. On behalf of the entire crew I apologize for the delay and also for the last minute gate change."

"Gate change?" I repeated.

I looked at Kyle, but he was already flipping through the in-flight magazine, ignoring the announcement. Then we all pushed back into our seats as the plane accelerated into take off.

"Thank you again," said the captain, "for choosing Brazilian Airways flight 455 nonstop to Rio de Janeiro."

NINE9

"Rio de Janeiro?!" I yelled.

The other passengers all turned to look at me and I offered an embarrassed 'I'm-not-crazy' smile.

"Yeah," said Kyle pointing inside the magazine without looking up, "there's a whole article in here about Carnival in Rio."

"That's because were going to Rio!" I hissed.

He looked at me with a puzzled expression. "Really? I thought the class trip was to Iceland this year."

"Right now, Kyle. Right now. We're flying to Rio de Janeiro right now."

His look only got more puzzled. "Jeni, Rio de Janeiro is in Brazil, not Japan."

"I know that," I growled through gritted teeth.

He raised his eyebrows and looked back at his article. "You don't seem like you do," he muttered.

I yanked the magazine out of his hands. "We got on the wrong plane, Kyle! We're not flying to Japan. We're flying to Brazil. We're on our way—nonstop I might add—to Rio de Janeiro, Brazil."

He looked at me for several seconds. Finally he said, "Oh. Well. That's bad."

I rolled my eyes and gave up on him. Instead, I craned my neck to see what Tommy was doing. Maybe he'd have an idea. But when I finally got a glimpse around the fat head of the man in front of me, all I saw was that Tommy's seat was empty. But when I flopped back in my seat, Tommy was standing next to me in the aisle.

"Oops," he observed.

I grimaced. "Yeah, oops. Late gate change, huh? Sorry."

He shrugged. "Nothing to be done about it now. I guess we won't have to wait so long for Ling after all. He'll probably even beat us there."

I felt acid dump into my stomach. This wasn't just a silly mix up. It was a disaster. Tommy was right, even if we hopped on the first plane out of Rio, it was still a thirteen-hour flight just to get there, plus who knows how many more to Tokyo. By the time it was all said and done, we were going to lose at least a day. And that would probably be enough to lose Nakajima. And that would mean we'd lose any chance of rescuing my mom.

Tommy must have seen the look on my face. He put a friendly hand on my shoulder. "It'll be okay. Try to get some rest. We'll get back on track as soon as we can."

I nodded but didn't try to say anything for fear I might start crying. He walked back toward his seat and I looked over at Kyle. He looked up from his magazine.

"It could be worse," he said.

"It could?" I doubted that.

"At least Miguel didn't catch us."

I smiled a little at that. "Thanks, Kyle. You always see the bright side."

I closed my eyes. It was early still, more dinner time than bed time, but the events of the last few hours had taken their toll. Before I even knew it, I was asleep.

TEN10

The flight to Rio sucked. I wanted to just sleep it away, but I kept having fretful dreams about gods and goddesses and missing moms and exploding houses. And every time I woke up Kyle was either sleeping peacefully, or reading some stupid article with a grin on his face. It was like he didn't even care at all.

It almost made me wish he hadn't come.

When the plane finally landed and we were at the gate, I couldn't wait to get off. Really. I got up first and pushed my way through all the travelers who actually had luggage. I was the first one off when the plane door opened and I went straight to the nearest monitor to figure out the next flight to Tokyo. Tommy and Kyle would just have to find me.

It took them a few minutes, and by then I'd found Japanese Airways flight 302 from Rio de Janeiro to Tokyo by way of Honolulu. It left in two hours. More than enough time to buy three tickets and get to the gate.

"Thanks for waiting for us," Kyle joked as they walked up. I ignored him.

"I found our flight," I announced. " Japanese Airways 302.

Leaves in two hours."

"Great," said Kyle. "I was already missing being jammed in an airplane seat for hours on end."

I ignored him again and looked at Tommy. He wasn't saying anything; he was just staring up at the screen.

"*Peso* for your thoughts," I said to him.

"Actually," interrupted Kyle, "Brazilian money is called *reals*."

And for the third time in as many minutes, I ignored him.

"All right then," Tommy finally said. "Let's get going. I've been here before so I know where to go."

I was quick to agree and fell in behind Tommy. Kyle stepped up next to me and we walked next to each other.

"Sorry about the *peso-real* comment," he said. "I can tell you're pretty upset."

"Can you blame me?" I answered. "My mom's been kidnapped and my house blew up. When we tried to get on a plane to save her, I got us on the wrong plane. *Really* wrong. We're not even on the right continent."

"We're not even in the right hemisphere," Kyle pointed out.

I glared at him. "Thanks."

"Sorry. They just pop into my head."

I shrugged. "It's okay. You're right. When I screw up, I screw up big. I mean, on my birthday, when something good is finally about to happen, when it turns out I'm supposed to become some reincarnated goddess, I screw that up too."

Kyle thought for a minute before responding. "Well, the wrong flight thing wasn't really your fault. We had Miguel Zapata chasing us—thanks to me—so we had to do something. In a way, getting on this plane was a success. We got away from Miguel."

"I guess," I shrugged. "But it won't get us to my mom any

faster."

"And the whole reincarnated goddess thing," Kyle went on, "That wasn't really your fault either. Your mom didn't tell you, so how were you supposed to know what was happening?"

"That's true," I admitted.

"I mean, jeez, you even peed your pants."

I stopped walking and looked at him. "I'm glad you keep reminding me of that."

I'd been so engrossed in talking with Kyle that I hadn't really been paying attention to where Tommy was taking us. Until we stepped through the doors and found ourselves outside.

"Is the Japanese Airways counter in a different terminal or something?" I asked him.

My question seemed to shake him out of a deep thought. "Hmm, what's that? Oh no. We're not going to Japanese Airways."

He made a gesture and the next taxi in the queue pulled up. "We're going into the city. Hop in."

ELEVEN11

I was livid. "Are you kidding me? Into the city? No! We have to get to Japan. We have to get there now. We have to get there yesterday!"

Tommy smiled. One of those smug, confident, smarmy smiles that makes you want to punch it right off the person's face. "Do you believe in fate, Jeni?"

I went from livid to apoplectic.

"You know," said Kyle, "that would have sounded even better if you'd used her last name." He lowered his voice, "'Do you believe in fate, Jeni Tanaka?' See?"

"Shut up, Kyle," I growled while still staring at Tommy. "I am not going into Rio de Janeiro. I am going back into this airport and taking flight 302 to Tokyo."

Tommy threw his hands up. "I don't even know if that's where she is."

My heart sank. "What?"

"I mean, that was my best guess," Tommy explained. "And it's probably right. But I don't really know."

I was stunned. I guess I hadn't really thought about it. I had just trusted him—trusted he knew what he was doing, where we were going, and why.

He saw the paralytic anger and fear in my eyes. "Now, we really can know. Gabriela can remote view."

"Who's Gabriela?" Kyle asked with a little too much interest.

"Gabriela is the godling to Odudawa, the Candomblé *orixa*—or spirit—of creation."

"The who of the what of the which?" I stuttered.

"Candomblé is a local religion," Tommy explained. "It combines many aspects of indigenous and African-immigrant spiritual traditions. It is this widespread connection of ancient traditions which enables Odudawa's godling to remote view."

"Okay." I crossed my arms. "And what's remote viewing?"

"Remote viewing is the ability to see things happening in far away places," Kyle explained. When I glared at him, he just shrugged. "I listen to a lot of late night radio."

"Gabriela will be able to tell us whether your mother is truly in Japan," Tommy added. "And if not, where she really is."

I was having trouble reconciling all this. One the one hand, it sounded ridiculous and a total waste of time. On the other hand, I was in the Rio de Janeiro airport with the godling to a Native American creation god, seeking my kidnapped mother who had been the godling to a Japanese creation goddess until it left her, attempted to enter me, and I rejected it, thereby potentially endangering all life on the planet.

I exhaled deeply. "Fate, huh?"

Tommy smiled. "Things happen for a reason. We were meant to get on that plane."

I shook my head. "I'm not sure I believe that. But at this point, maybe I'll go ahead and believe anything."

I stepped forward and opened the taxi door. "Fine. Let's go

find Gabriela."

Tommy smiled and slapped Kyle on the back, causing him to stumble slightly. "Your friend is wise, Kyle."

Kyle regained his balance. "See, again that would have been better as 'Your friend is wise, Kyle Emerson.'"

"Kyle?" I said, as I sat down in the taxi.

"Yes?"

"Shut up and get in."

TWELVE12

The drive into downtown Rio de Janeiro was uneventful. No one felt like talking.

Well, okay, *I* didn't feel like talking.

And the dark cloud over my head scared Tommy and Kyle into respectful, or maybe fearful, silence. I just stared intently out the car window. I was on the fence between angry and resigned. They didn't want to say anything that might push me the wrong way.

It worked. By the time we'd reached Gabriela's neighborhood, I'd had the chance to process everything, at least a little bit. Tommy was right. It made more sense to get some guidance on where to look, rather than just rush to the most likely spot.

"Did you hear the one about the man looking for a quarter on the sidewalk?" I asked while still looking out the car window.

When there wasn't an immediate reply, I turned to my traveling companions. Kyle was looking at me like I was crazy, but Tommy was letting a smile creep into the corner of his mouth.

"No," said Tommy. "What about him?"

"Well," I said, "he's down on his hands and knees looking for it when another man walks by and asks him what he's doing. He tells him he's looking for a quarter he dropped. The other man is a nice guy so he gets down on his hands and knees too and starts looking. After a few minutes of not finding the quarter, the second man asks the first man where he dropped the quarter. 'On fifth street,' the first man says. The second man is stunned. 'But this is Fourth Street,' he says. 'Yeah,' says the first man, 'but the light is better over here.'"

Kyle still looked like he thought I was crazy, but Tommy got it.

The taxi pulled to a stop in front of Gabriela's apartment building.

"Come on," Tommy said opening the taxi door. "Let's find out what street your mom is on."

Kyle stumbled out after us and looked up at the street sign. "It looks like this is *Rua Marquês*."

Tommy and I both ignored him and he ran to catch up with us at the front door. There was no lobby, just a security door with a posted list of tenant names and number codes.

Tommy pointed to the listing 'G. Paiz 35.' "Here we are."

"She has her own apartment?" I was surprised. "So she's not a teenager like us?"

"Oh, she's a teenager all right," Tommy replied, pressing the 3 and 5 on the key pad, "but she's been on her own for a while. Not everyone grows up with backyards and minivans."

I tried to figure out if Tommy had just insulted me while we waited for a reply from Gabriela. After a minute of silence, Tommy tried again. Then a third time. Nothing.

"Now what?" I complained.

Tommy just shook his head and looked around for some

other entrance.

Kyle stepped forward and pressed the number pad, seemingly at random. I watched him, then looked at Tommy who only shrugged and shook his head slightly.

"*Sim? Olá?*" came a female voice over the speaker.

"*Olá. Este é Pãolo,*" Kyle said into the squawk box. "*Eu deixei minhas calças no apartamento de Ana. Você pode me deixar entrar, por favor?*"

Without hesitation the person on the other end buzzed the door open and we were inside.

"You speak Brazilian?" I was stunned.

"Portuguese," he corrected. "And yeah, a little. I needed to learn some for capoeira and I just went ahead and taught myself some more."

I was still stunned. "What did you say?"

"I told her my name was Pãolo and I had left my pants in Ana's apartment and could she please buzz me in."

"Who's Ana?"

Kyle laughed. "I don't know, but it's one of the most common girls names in Brazil. I figured there was probably one in the building. Pãolo is pretty common too."

I shook my head and gave him a soft punch on the arm. "You surprise me sometimes, Kyle Emerson."

He laughed. "See? That sounded great."

"Yes, well," Tommy interrupted and cleared his throat. "We should get on up to Gabriela's apartment. It's on the third floor."

"Okay," Kyle and I said in unison and we followed our new friend up a narrow, musty staircase to the third floor.

Tommy rapped on the door, but when he did, it just swung open. A quick look inside revealed that the place had been ransacked. Furniture was overturned, cushions and pillows were strewn across the floor, papers and baubles had been tossed every which way. Tommy took a single step inside.

"Gabriela?" he called out. "Gabriela?"

There was no answer.

"We should call the police," Kyle suggested.

"I'm not so sure," I replied. "Three American teenagers and a missing Brazilian with a ransacked house. I'd hate for them to suspect us."

"Why would we burglarize Gabriela's apartment?" Kyle said, using her first name like he was friends with her already. "You and I have never even met her. It's not like we know she's got valuables or something."

Tommy's eyes widened at the word 'valuables.' "No!"

He ran inside, toward a back bedroom. We heard some stuff being stepped on and thrown around, and then another, louder "No!"

We ran in and saw Tommy staring into an empty jewelry box on what was presumably Gabriela's dresser.

"It's gone," he gasped. "Whoever did this, they took her talisman. We're doomed."

THIRTEEN13

"Talisman?" I said.

"Doomed?" asked Kyle.

Tommy threw a frantic look around the room, then shook the jewelry box as if the missing object might fall out of it.

"Gabriela's talisman. It's an ancient Candomblé artifact, a symbol of the power of Odudawa."

"Doomed?" Kyle whispered again to me. I hushed him with a stern glance.

"Not, not a symbol," Tommy corrected himself. "A totem. Her connection to her god."

He reached into his shirt and pulled out a leather strap with a carved stone bear attached. "We each have one. Mine is ancient, handed down from father to son, parent to child for generations. It is a totem for my creation spirit."

"Did my mom have one too?" I felt stupid asking a stranger about my own mother. "I mean, if she did, I never noticed it. I don't think she went around wearing some talisman pendant. I think I would have noticed that."

Tommy shook his head and squeezed the stone bear in his

hand. "No, everyone's totem is different. Mine is small enough to be worn as a necklace. Gabriela's was a necklace too, but it was huge. Far too big to wear all the time."

He looked at the jewelry box. "She usually kept it here. I don't know what your mother's totem was. Everyone had one but it's not like we sat around and compared them at a Tupperware party."

"Totem-ware," Kyle joked. When I glared at him, his eyes widened again and he whispered, "Doomed?"

"Kyle has a point," I finally admitted. "Why are we doomed?"

Tommy's face looked genuinely concerned, frightened even. "If Nakajima is collecting our totems it means this is bigger than just playing against his rival. He might be trying to gather all the gods' powers to himself. The totems can act as a gateway to the spirits. If he can gather all the totems, he might be able to gather all the spirits together. If he does that, who knows what he might do."

It was so much to try to understand. Whenever it started to seem too big for me, I just thought of my mom. "Well, totems or not, we need to find Gabriela so she can tell me where my mom is."

I looked around the room. "Do you think they kidnapped Gabriela too?"

Tommy shrugged. "Maybe. Or maybe this was a burglary while she was out."

That made sense. "Okay, why don't you two look in here for some clue as to where she might be," I said. "I'll check out front. If I find something I'll holler."

"'Holler'?" Kyle teased. "Nice word."

"Yes," I said with exaggerated dignity. "Holler."

I walked back out to the front room of the apartment. I wasn't exactly sure what I was looking for, but I hoped I'd know it when I saw it. I just didn't expect the what to be a who.

After a minute or two of scanning the debris strewn across the room, the front door swung open and a very tall woman with very long hair stood in the doorway, her eyes burning as she surveyed the wreckage. Before I could say anything, she jumped and grabbed me by the hair. A second later I'd been thrown flat on my face, both of my arms twisted up behind me and a forearm across the back of my neck.

"*Quem é você?*" she hissed in my ear.

"Holler!" I, well, hollered.

FOURTEEN14

It seemed like forever until Kyle and Tommy finally sauntered out of the bedroom to find me helpless on the floor beneath my gigantic assailant.

"Did you find someth—?" Tommy started as he stepped through the door.

Kyle was right behind him, but as soon as he saw me he shrieked, "Let go of her!" and pushed Tommy aside.

He ran up to my attacker and took his ready capoeira stance. I mentally rolled my eyes, but then I could feel her release her hold on me and slowly rise up to square off with Kyle. She started to take a similar stance, but Kyle dropped down and tried to surprise her with a sweep kick, intended to knock her off her feet. She'd seen it coming and jumped just in time for Kyle's leg to pass harmlessly underneath.

But the kick swung his body into just the right position to land a second kick against her hip and she was sent tumbling.

I was impressed. I'd never seen Kyle really fight before, just demonstration exercises. It had always looked more like dancing than fighting.

Kyle bounced and bobbed up to the woman where she had landed, but she managed to push herself up into a handstand and land a full body kick against his chest.

I winced at the force of the blow as Kyle went crashing into a pile of junk in the kitchen. He had the wind knocked out of him and was gasping for breath as the tall brunette danced toward him, a smile on her face and her hands in fists.

Kyle scrambled back onto his feet and was able to get into a ready position before she managed another strike. In fact, it seemed like she gave him time to get up. Then she threw a punch and a kick, both of which Kyle successfully blocked. He threw a counter kick, which she blocked, then she connected with a kick to his upper arm. It knocked him over and she stepped in for another strike, but he pushed himself up onto his hands and nailed her with a roundhouse kick to her back. She went flying into the wall and Kyle followed it up with that leg sweep he'd missed before. He knocked her feet out from under her and she crashed to the ground.

He dropped onto her to pin her, but then she used her size to flip him around and ended up sitting on his chest, his shirt collar in one hand and a fist raised above his face.

"Enough, Gabriela," said Tommy. "He's a friend."

"Gabriela?" I shouted at Tommy. "This is Gabriela? Why didn't you stop them?"

Tommy smiled. "Did you want to stop, Gabriela?"

She smiled, her full lips spreading across her pretty face. "No, Thomas. It has been a long time since I have enjoyed such an opponent."

"How about you, Kyle?" Tommy asked.

Kyle looked up the beautiful and powerful woman sitting inches from his face. "Uhhh," was all he could say.

Gabriela unclenched her fist and pulled Kyle's head up by

the shirt collar to kiss his cheek. "You fight well, boy. Where did you learn capoeira?"

"Seattle Capoeira Academy," he replied in a daze. "I have a blue belt."

Gabriela's smile broadened even further. "I have a red belt." Then her voice lowered to a throaty purr. "Perhaps I can teach you some things."

Kyle turned red, but not as red as I was turning.

"Ahem," I growled. "Aren't you going to introduce us to my attacker, Tommy?"

Tommy smiled. "Gabriela Paiz, godling to Odudawa, I'd like you to meet Jeni Tanaka, godling to Izamani no Mikoto. Or at least she was supposed to be. That's why we're here."

Gabriela grasped Kyle's hand then sprang off of him, pulling him to his feet all in one fluid motion. "I know why you are here. Everyone knows how she has made a mess of things."

"Hey!" I yelled. "I didn't know—"

But she wasn't even listening to me. Instead she asked Kyle, "Is she your girlfriend?"

Kyle stammered, "Uh, uh, no. Not, er... No."

Another full lipped smile. "Good."

"We need your help, Gabriela," Tommy said. "To find out where Nakajima took Jeni's mother."

Gabriela Paiz stepped over and looked down at me. She circled me as I stood in her ransacked living room and appraised me like a dog at the pound. When she'd completed a circle and was standing in front of me again, she turned away and closed her eyes.

"No, I will not help her. I reject her as the godling to Izamani no Mikoto."

FIFTEEN15

"Reject me?" I'd had enough of Miss Tall-and-Mighty. "Who are *you* to reject *me*?"

She turned her head and glared down at me. "*I* am the godling to Odudawa. And *you* are nothing."

I was so angry I couldn't think.

"No, you are worse than nothing," she snarled. "You have ruined everything. You have imperiled everything."

"And I'm here to fix it," I shot back. "Tommy said you could help, so help."

She was a bit taken aback, but wasn't about to be swayed by one sharp sentence. "You misunderstand me, little girl. We are in danger because of your reckless actions. I am not certain it is wise to help you. Perhaps you are not fated to be Izamani's godling."

Tommy looked like he was about to say something but I glared at him and cut a hand toward him. I could handle this myself, thank you.

"You mean," I asked, "because I made a mistake that endangered the delicate balance between good and evil, creation and destruction?"

"Exactly," sneered Gabriela.

I grinned and jerked my thumb toward her bedroom. "Well, then you might need to draft up a resignation letter yourself, missy, because you left your totem out where the bad guys could find it, and now it's gone."

Gabriela's smug expression shattered and she spun to look at Tommy. He gave a confirmatory shrug. Her eyes flared and she bolted past him, leaping over the broken debris covering the floor.

It only took a few seconds until we heard her cry, "No!" then throw the jewelry box against the wall. After a few more moments she staggered out again and leaned against the doorframe.

"What does it mean, Thomas?" she asked weakly.

"It means Nakajima isn't satisfied with just Shinigami and Izamani. He plans to take all the spirits." He walked over to her and placed a hand on her shoulder. "And it means we're running out of time."

She looked at him for a moment then over at me. "All right, little one. I will help you."

SIXTEEN16

We all cleared space at Gabriela's dining room table. Kyle tried to carefully set the clutter into safe spots on the floor, but everyone else, including Gabriela, simply swept the trash onto the floor then kicked it aside. In a few moments we were seated around the table.

"I need something of your mother's," Gabriela announced.

I hesitated. "I— I don't think I have anything." I tried to think what I might have of hers. "My house kinda blew up."

Gabriela sighed and gave Tommy a pained expression. He patted her hand encouragingly.

"Do you have anything at all?" she asked. "Even just something she may have touched. There are billions upon billions of souls on this planet. It can be difficult to isolate one of them without some reference."

"Maybe in your purse?" Kyle suggested.

I shrugged and walked over to where I'd set my purse when we'd first arrived in the ransacked apartment. I dug through it. Lipstick? No. House keys? Maybe. MP3 player? Worth a try.

I held up the player. "My mom gave me this for my birthday

last year. Is that good enough?"

"It will have to be," Gabriela sighed.

I handed her the player and sat down again. She examined it, holding it up and pressing buttons. Finally she said, "I don't like your taste in music either."

I started to stand up, but Kyle placed a hand on my arm. He turned to Gabriela. "Show us what else you can do, Gabriela."

She smiled at the flattery. Then she turned and gave me a teasing wink, before setting the MP3 player on the table in front of her. Reaching out her hands, she rested her long red fingernails on top of the device, and looked up, her eyes closing.

Then suddenly she slumped onto the table with a meaty thwack as her head hit her arm. I started to get up again, this time to help her, but Tommy stopped me with a curt wave and a shake of his head.

Gabriela lay there for the longest time. I looked at Kyle. He looked at me, then at Tommy. Tommy looked back at him, then at me. I looked at Kyle again and we both shrugged. Tommy just closed his eyes and waited.

Finally, Gabriela's head popped back up.

"Shanghai!" she shouted. "Your mother is in Shanghai!"

SEVENTEEN17

"Shanghai?" I was stunned. "Isn't that where, um, Ting-Lau—?"

"Ling Tau," Tommy corrected.

"Right. Isn't that where Ling Tau is?"

Tommy frowned as he considered. "It's where he lives. But remember, we called him away. He's on his way to Japan even now."

"What's his totem?" Kyle realized to ask.

Gabriela and Tommy frowned at each other.

"It's not jewelry," Tommy said. "He never wears any jewelry."

"It must be something else," Gabriela said unnecessarily.

"Is it portable?" I posed the key question. "Would he have taken it with him?"

Tommy's eyes widened in realization. "Maybe. Gabriela, have you ever been to his home in Shanghai?"

"No," she answered. "He visited me here once but I've never been there. Why?"

"His apartment is exquisitely decorated, and the centerpiece of the living room is a three foot long jade dragon. I bet that's his totem."

"Too big to take with him," Kyle started.

"But small enough for Nakajima to steal," I finished.

"And we're the ones who got him to leave," Tommy added. "I'd say we need to go there right away, but Nakajima's already a step a head of us. We'd probably get there just as he left. We should try to guess his next move and head him off there."

"Uh, hello?" I stood up from the table. "Don't forget about my mother. She's in Shanghai so that's where we're going."

"He'll probably take her with him to his next stop, whatever that is," Tommy offered.

"Probably?" I repeated.

Tommy shrugged.

"We should go to Shanghai," Kyle said, also standing. "That's where she is now. A bird in the hand is worth two in the bush."

"This bird isn't in hand," Tommy argued. "At best, it's in a bush across the Pacific Ocean. And I still think by the time we get there, that bird will have flown."

This was pointless. "Tommy," I reminded him, "you said Gabriela would tell us where my mom is so we could go there. Well, she said she's in Shanghai, so I'm going to Shanghai."

"Me too," agreed Kyle.

Gabriela stood up and looped her arm through Kyle's. "Then I will go with you as well."

EIGHTEEN18

Somehow, that surprised me. It surprised Kyle too, I think, but he did a terrible job of hiding his pleasure at it. He just looked at her arm, then at her face, and then at the floor, his face flushing.

"Are you sure, Gabriela?" I tried. "This isn't really your fight."

She held Kyle's arm tighter. "Oh, but it is. Your error has endangered us all. This fight is all of ours now."

I tried to smile, but I'm pretty sure I failed. I could tell she was going to hold the whole 'you've endangered us all' thing over my head as long as she could. I was so glad she was coming with us—not.

"Besides," she said waving her free arm at the carnage around us. "I can't stay here. It's not safe anymore. I want to find my talisman as much as you want to find your mother."

I raised an eyebrow at her.

"Perhaps not quite as much as that," she conceded. "Nevertheless, I would feel useless here."

All eyes turned to Tommy, still seated at the table. "All right," he said, pushing himself up from the table like an old man,

"I'm in too. But I bet we just miss him again."

"All the more reason to hurry," I urged. "Where can we get a taxi?"

"No need," answered Gabriela. "I have a car. It is small, but Kyle and I can squish in the back."

My eyes narrowed. This was going to be very irritating, especially if Kyle kept grinning like that.

We all started to get up from the table, and I was so annoyed with Kyle that I didn't notice it at first.

"Brr," said Kyle. "Did you feel that?"

I had, but it didn't register. It should have, though. A cold blast of air on a hot Brazilian afternoon.

I looked at the others. Kyle was looking out the window to see if it had come from there. Tommy and Gabriela were looking at each other, like they knew what was going on. And behind all of them was a swirling vapor filling the kitchen.

I pointed at the materializing wraith, but could only manage to say, "Gkk—!"

Tommy and Gabriela turned and saw it. They froze for a second while Kyle turned around too.

He screamed. Like a girl. And I know because I screamed too.

The swirling cloud had constituted itself into a floating ghost. A woman, I think. With empty eyes and a grotesquely warped open mouth. The faint moan emanating from her suddenly transformed into a shriek—as she shot past the others right toward me!

Tommy reacted like lightning and tackled me just in time. The spirit raced over me and circled up to the ceiling for another pass.

"Quickly!" shouted Gabriela, grabbing my arms and pulling

both me and Kyle out into hallway. "Thomas will hold her off."

I looked back to see Tommy standing in the doorway, his bear totem off his neck and in his hands, held up as a weapon against the swirling wraith. The spirit looked angry and about ready to charge him, but I didn't get to see anymore because Gabriela pulled me and Kyle into the stairwell and we ran down the stairs as fast as we could.

NINETEEN19

Gabriela, Kyle, and I spilled out onto the humid street and tried to get our bearings. Gabriela looked around for the briefest second then yanked us again in some unknown—to me and Kyle anyway—direction.

As we ran-stumbled after her, I tried to look back for Tommy. I hoped he was okay. I hoped he knew what he was doing. I hoped I'd see him again.

I wasn't really paying attention to where we were going, but in a minute or two we found ourselves in Gabriela's car. It was about the size of a golf cart. A small golf cart. She jumped in the driver's seat and started it. Kyle and I knew enough to jump in after her. In a moment she was tearing out of the garage and around the corner in front of her apartment complex.

She screeched the car to a halt right by the front door. "Come on, Thomas," she said, tapping the steering wheel.

"Come on, Tommy," I repeated to myself. It seemed like the spirit was after me. I couldn't believe he would stand up to it for me. It made me want to see him again all the more.

It turned out I didn't have to wait long. Tommy opened the

apartment building's front door and casually stepped outside. Without really realizing what I was doing, I jumped out of the alleged car and ran up to him. I threw myself around him.

"You're okay!" I shouted.

After an awkward moment or two, he hugged me back. "Y— Yes. I'm okay."

I pulled away from the hug to look him in the face. "Thank you."

He looked me right in the eye. "Of course, Jeni."

His arms felt so good around my waist. So of course Kyle jumped in.

"What was that thing?" Kyle shouted from the car.

"A doppelganger of Exu," Tommy answered. "The Candomblé spirit of destruction. The godling can astrally project an aspect of the god. Normally it would be powerless against Gabriela, but—"

"It must have known Gabriela lost her totem," I finished.

"So I guess we know who's responsible for the theft," Kyle said.

I was a little disappointed that I wasn't the target of the wraith after all. I had felt important for a moment. I still felt a little important, though. Tommy hadn't let go of my waist.

"Come along, you two," Gabriela barked. "We should get to the airport."

God, I really hated her.

TWENTY20

We made it to the airport quickly enough and had no trouble getting our tickets to Shanghai. It was a long flight, with a stop in Hawaii, but it was the same flight route as the last flight to Shanghai and was only three hours after it. We figured if Nakajima was on that flight, we'd only be three hours behind him.

We had some time to kill before the flight, and there didn't appear to be any Aztec gods of destruction following us, so I walked around a bit looking at the planes and people and shops and whatever I rested my tired eyes on. I might as well— Kyle was busy with Miss Brazil. They had gone off on a walk of their own. I wouldn't have gone with them, but I was kinda mad they didn't ask me to. When I circled back to the waiting area for our flight, Tommy was playing on his cell phone.

I plopped down in the seat next to him. "Whatcha doin'?"

He tapped the screen, dimming it. "Trying to get a hold of Ling, but no luck. He's not answering his phone."

"He's probably in the air somewhere."

"Yeah, probably," Tommy nodded. "So I just sent him a text. He'll get it when he lands."

Tommy slid the phone into his pants pocket.

"I hope this works out," he said. "I hate just chasing after Nakajima. I want to head him off."

I avoided the obvious 'head 'em off at the pass' Indian joke. Instead I said, "At least we're not in Japan. We're already closer to him than he expected. Maybe we're making him sweat a little bit."

Tommy smiled. "I like that. See, now I feel better. I guess it's good we came to Rio."

"Do you believe in fate, Thomas Bluehorse?" I joked.

We both laughed just as Kyle and Queen Amazonia walked up.

"What's so funny?" Kyle asked.

"Aw, nothing," I answered.

"Inside joke," Tommy explained.

Kyle's smile weakened a little. "Oh," was all he managed to say. And we all were pretty quiet after that as we waited to board our slow plane to China.

TWENTY-ONE21

We couldn't get four seats together, so I sat alone near a wing, Tommy sat on the other side and Kyle and the man-eater sat together in the back. I spent most of the trip either trying to figure out was going on, or trying to forget that it was. When we got to Honolulu the older lady who was sitting next to me got off and I thought I might get to have an empty seat for the rest of the trip.

No such luck. A girl about my age plopped down next to me without so much as a 'Hello.' She just looked at me once, made sure I read her disapproval, then slipped her ear-buds in and ignored me. Just as well, I figured.

She never said a word to me, even when I had to get past her to use the bathroom. It made me feel even more alone. I was relieved when the pilot announced the descent toward the Shanghai airport, but I was nervous somehow about talking to Tommy again, and I just didn't want to see Kyle and his new girlfriend. I slowly put my things away and waited for the landing.

As the plane bounced on the ground and we all slammed back against our seats from the pilot throwing up the flaps and hitting the brakes, Ms. I-Don't-Want-To-Talk-To-You pulled her ear-buds out by their cords and said, without looking at me, "I know who you are."

I was beyond surprised. "How—? I mean—"

"Don't say anything." She bent down and pretended to be repacking her carry-on bag. "You don't want them to know I talked to you. I don't know everything they've told you, but I know not all of it is true. Be careful whom you trust. You can't afford to make a mistake."

By then the plane had come to a stop and she stood up and disappeared through the curtain to the first class section. I thought about getting up to follow her, but the stewardess came by reminding everyone to stay seated until the plane arrived at the gate. By the time I was able to get off the plane, the girl was long gone.

"Good flight?" Tommy asked as he walked up to join me.

Before I could even figure out how, or whether, to answer, Kyle and Gabriela walked up.

"Did you know Gabriela is a Capricorn?" Kyle asked. "And I'm a Virgo? Isn't that amazing?"

I was about to say something I would regret when a twenty-year-old Chinese man, with chiseled features and dressed perfectly from head to toe, stormed up to us and shouted, "What the hell are you doing here?!"

TWENTY-TWO22

I offered my hand in greeting. "Ling Tau, I presume."

He looked at my hand, then ignored me to address Tommy. "I am serious, Bluehorse. Why are you in my city?"

"Did you get my text?" Tommy asked.

"Of course I got your text. How else would I know to be at the airport?"

Tommy stood up straighter against the verbal onslaught. "Then you know why we're in your city."

Ling's eyes narrowed. He scanned our group. He gave Gabriela an acknowledging grunt, and sniffed at Kyle. Then he rested his gaze on me.

"You are the cause of our current crisis, I take it?"

"I'm Jeni Tanaka," I answered. "And I'm not the cause of anything. I'm the solution."

It sounded good, but I was just blustering. Even though I knew it wasn't really my fault that I'd endangered the world, I also knew that I had, in fact, done so. So while I claimed to be the solution, I knew I'd be fixing my own mistake.

Ling Tau clearly understood it too. He shook his head dismissively at me and turned back to Tommy.

"You shouldn't be here. Nakajima isn't here. You should have gone to Japan like we originally agreed."

"But my mom is here," I interjected. "At least that's what Gabriela says."

"It is true," the Brazilian agreed. "Her mother is here in Shanghai."

"This isn't about her mother!" Ling snapped. "It's about us, the spirits we honor, and the end of everything."

"But my mom—"

"I don't care one bit about your mother," Ling hissed at me. "I care about stopping Nakajima before he destroys everything."

Tommy stepped over and laid a hand on Ling's shoulder, something Ling clearly was uncomfortable with. "Let's all calm down and take this conversation someplace more private. People are starting to stare. We don't need extra attention right now."

Sure enough, some nearby travelers were examining this group of teenagers from different countries hissing and hushing at one another.

"Let's go back to your place, Ling Tau," Tommy suggested. "We can discuss matters more freely there."

Ling became visibly rigid at the suggestion he take us back to his apartment. He took several moments to formulate a response.

"I do not think it wise for you to stay in Shanghai for any period of time. You should leave here as soon as possible. You will accomplish nothing here."

"Then it's settled," Gabriela announced with a broad smile. "If you think we should not go to your home, then I am convinced it is the right thing to do."

She slapped him on the back, then stepped past him towards

the exit. "Where did you park?"

So Gabriela and Ling didn't like each other. Good. I smiled at Kyle as the enemy of my enemy became my friend.

TWENTY-THREE23

"Nice digs," said Kyle as we stepped into Ling's apartment.

I would have agreed but my breath was taken away by the perfect awesomeness of the decorating. Or awesome perfection. Not sure which. But it was awesome and it was perfect.

Traditional Chinese art paintings hung on the walls, and the shelves and cabinets held sculptures and artifacts of every shape and kind. But everything in the room, from the furniture to the paintings to the carpets to even the light switch covers, framed and directed the eye to the centerpiece on the mantel: an exquisite jade sculpture of an Eastern dragon, spinning and wrapping itself around its own body in an endlessly graceful knot.

"Wow," I finally said.

And for the first time Ling smiled. "Yes. You are correct."

So he was modest too. Glad to know he was the leader of this new group I was supposed to be in. I was almost glad I had screwed up the initiation.

Almost.

We all took seats in the black leather couches surrounding the burgundy-stained bamboo coffee table. Kyle and Gabriela were next to each other on one side, Tommy and I on the other, and Ling sat in a leather chair at the head of the table. Seemed about right.

"We need to tell you about what happened to Gabriela," Tommy started.

"I know what happened to Gabriela," Ling interrupted. "Her totem was stolen."

"So you understand the urgency," Tommy pressed. "Nakajima is collecting our totems. He intends to steal all of our spirits."

"Not necessarily," Ling countered. He pointed at the jade dragon behind him. "My totem is safe, as is yours. It could simply be a coincidence. Perhaps Gabriela's apartment was simply burglarized and they stumbled upon the necklace. I have seen it. At first glance it appears quite valuable."

"It *is* quite valuable," Gabriela understood Ling's veiled insult. "And it was the only thing taken. My home was ransacked. They went through everything to find that talisman."

Ling smiled again, but it was a cold, challenging smile. "Then you should have hidden it better."

"Said the man who built a display cabinet for his totem," Kyle muttered, waving at the jade dragon.

Ling's smile snapped off his face and he stared at Kyle for several seconds. "Who are you again, boy?"

"Kyle Emerson." His voice was pretty steady, all things considered.

I was about to say 'He's my friend' because that would have been so impressive coming from me, but Brazilia beat me to it.

"He is my friend, Ling," she said. "Treat him accordingly."

I wasn't sure what Ling would consider appropriate treatment for Gabriela, but it was probably better than how he'd treat me. Kyle was moving up in the world.

I slumped back into the couch. At least Tommy seemed to notice.

"Well, we should probably figure out our next step," he said. "Jeni's mom is somewhere in Shanghai, probably with Nakajima. If we can find her, we'll find him, and Gabriela's totem."

"He is not here," Ling assured, but again without explaining his certainty. "And first thing is first. It is dinner time. We can discuss this while we eat."

I was a bit surprised to hear it was dinner time. On the other hand, I had no idea of what time it was. I'd spent the last day flying over three continents and the planet's biggest ocean. I think it was tomorrow already. Maybe even the day after tomorrow. I decided I could eat. Especially Chinese food.

Ling didn't wait for an answer, but instead pulled out his cell phone—the latest model, of course—and tapped the screen a few times. Then he said something into the phone in Chinese and hung up again. I wasn't surprised he didn't ask us what we wanted.

"There is a restaurant around the corner," he explained. "The best in Shanghai. Our order will be ready in ten minutes."

Then a twinkle shot across his eyes. "Why don't you go pick it up, Kyle Emerson? We godlings need a chance to talk. Alone."

I was actually kind of glad to be included in the whole godling club, although I felt a little bad for Kyle. Then I remembered my birthday party and I felt even worse. I was about to volunteer to go with him, maybe make some comment about not really being a godling, not yet anyway, but Gabriela beat me to it again.

"I will go with him," she announced. "You do not need me to discuss rescuing Jeni's mother."

Kyle, who had been a bit stunned by Ling's order, suddenly perked up. "Sounds good. I can't wait to see Shanghai at night."

There was something about that comment and his oblivious attitude that reminded me of the other definition of "shanghai": to get shanghaied, or kidnapped. I should have said something, but ever since Gabriela had kicked his butt he was really irritating to be around. Besides, now I really was important, meeting with just our leader and Tommy.

As the door shut behind Kyle and Gabriela, I felt confident enough to say something, "If Nakajima really is stealing totems, why do you suppose he still has my mother?"

Ling sneered. "This just proves my point. He is not stealing totems. And he is not in Shanghai."

"Gabriela says he is," I countered.

"Gabriela is a fool! She—"

"She is our friend," chided Tommy. He had stood up and was admiring Ling's collections. He didn't bother looking at us as he spoke. "Each of us brings a unique perspective. That is our strength. We each see things the others cannot."

Ling scoffed. "Platitudes. Beautiful and empty."

"Don't be so sure, Ling Tau," said Tommy as he reached the jade dragon. "For example, as I lay my eyes upon your precious dragon totem I can see something you cannot."

Ling spun around in his chair. "What is that?"

Tommy picked up the statue and smashed it against the shelf, shattering the expertly painted plaster.

"This is a fake. Nakajima already has your totem."

TWENTY-FOUR24

Ling sprang from his chair and scooped up the counterfeit plaster in his manicured hands. "How can this be?!"

"Looks like you need to upgrade the security system," I said. "Now do you believe us?"

"Silence!" Ling threw the plaster pieces to the floor, shattering them even further. "I will not be lectured by you who caused this!"

"Ling..." Tommy started but I interrupted.

"You don't have to stand up for me anymore, Tommy." I turned to our host. "Ling, you need to adjust your attitude. You may be the oldest, but that doesn't mean you know everything."

"You'd be surprised by what I know," he growled.

"Or maybe I wouldn't," I shot back. I pointed to the broken fake totem. "But obviously you don't know everything. So maybe you should step back a bit and be open to the possibility that somebody somewhere might have more information than you."

I'd just met him so it was hard to say for sure, but I don't think he could have looked any angrier. I suddenly wished Kyle were there with his stupid capoeira moves. Gabriela would probably help him, so even if Ling knew kung fu or something, it would still be two against one.

Tommy could see the red flare in Ling's eyes too. "We should contact the others," he said, changing the subject slightly. "Let them know to guard their totems, and find out if anyone else has had theirs stolen."

Ling didn't respond. He was still staring at me. He hadn't replied to my admonition. Instead he was trying to stare me down. But I held his gaze. I wasn't going to blink first, damn it.

"Have you seen my phone?" I heard Tommy ask, but I didn't break off from Ling to respond.

A minute later Tommy asked again, his voice more concerned. "No, really. I can't find my phone."

Ling's face contorted a bit, but he didn't want to give up the staring contest either.

Tommy finally stepped between us. "Will you two knock it off? This is serious. My phone is missing."

"So what?" I was irritated he interrupted my attempt to out-intimidate Ling.

"So it has all the information on all of us. And now, somehow, *they* have it."

TWENTY-FIVE25

"How do you know they have it?" I asked. "Maybe you just lost it."

"They have it," agreed Ling. "It will be impossible to withstand what is coming if you two keep making mistakes like this."

"Us two?" Tommy took umbrage of being lumped in with me. I couldn't help but notice. "This wasn't a mistake."

"What would you call it, Bluehorse?" Ling crossed his arms.

"I'd call it theft," he answered. "It's not a mistake if someone steals something from me."

"It's a mistake to allow that to happen to something you know is important."

I jerked a thumb toward the plaster shards behind him. "How's that totem of yours, Ling?"

Tommy didn't even try to suppress his laugh. "She's got you there, Ling."

Ling lowered his eyebrows. "I'm sure she doesn't. That is something else entirely."

"So what's the big deal about losing your phone?" I asked

Tommy.

"It has all of our personal information, including what each person's totem is. At least to the extent I know."

I shrugged. "It sure seems to me like everybody knows everybody. There's only twelve of you right?"

"Eleven," Ling hissed.

I winced. "Right, eleven."

"Plus the twelve on the other side," Tommy added.

"Okay, so twenty-four—"

"Twenty-three," Ling interjected again.

"Twenty-three," I sighed. "If you know everything, I bet they do too."

Tommy ran a hand through his thick, black hair. "No, that's the point. I don't know everything. I'd worked really hard to gather as much information as I could, but not everybody is as open as Gabriela and me."

"Not everyone is as reckless as you and Gabriela, you mean," said Ling. He was a real downer.

Tommy didn't take the bait. "Anyway, it's got everything I could figure out from as many of us, and them, as I could."

A thought struck me. "The godling to the Brazilian god of destruction, she isn't a teenage girl by any chance, is she?"

"Candomblé, not Brazilian," Tommy corrected. He shrugged. "I don't know. That was one of the ones I was working on."

"Does Gabriela know?" I asked.

"I don't think so. The spirit had recently transferred, and we were still trying to figure out who the new godling was."

My mind raced as I considered the girl on the plane and Gabriela and Kyle. Then I realized something.

"Shouldn't they be back with the food by now?"

Tommy looked at his watch. "It has been a while," he agreed.

"Call them," I suggested without thinking.

Tommy glared at me with his palms up.

"Right," I laughed. "No phone."

"I will call the restaurant," Ling snapped.

He slipped his phone out of his pocket and tapped it a couple of times before placing it against his ear and half-yelling into it several times. He finished with a "*Xièxiè*" then lowered the phone.

"They never made it there."

TWENTY-SIX26

Shanghai's night streets were illuminated by a million bulbs of every type and color. But there were still plenty of dark cracks for light-averse vermin. And that's where we found ourselves within minutes of rushing out of Ling's apartment. After a quick stop at the restaurant to confirm Kyle and Gabriela had never made it there, Ling led us down several streets and alleyways until we found ourselves in a dirty, smelly back alley some unknown distance and direction from his flat.

"We're getting nowhere," Tommy complained. "They could be anywhere. This is a huge city."

"They can't be that far away," Ling argued. "They are on foot and they don't speak Mandarin."

I raised a finger. "How do you know Kyle doesn't speak Mandarin?"

"Does he?"

"Well, no," I admitted, "but he could."

Ling closed his eyes and took in a sharp, deep breath. "We should split up."

Tommy frowned. "Are you sure that's wise? If someone

abducted them—"

"Then they have their hands full with the two of them," Ling interrupted, "and they will be in no position to resist even one of us."

I wasn't sure I agreed with that logic, but Tommy gave in.

"Okay," he said. "We'll all split up and meet back at the restaurant in fifteen minutes."

"Thirty," ordered Ling. "And Jeni will come with me."

Tommy's head jerked up almost as sharply as mine.

"What?" we both said, before then both asking, "Why?"

"You have been here before, Bluehorse," he answered, "and I trust you to take care of yourself. I do not trust her."

"Thanks," I sneered.

Ling ignored me. "Although I doubt she will live up to being the next godling to Izamani no Mikoto, she is currently too valuable to leave alone. If Nakajima gets her, he may well be able to lure Izamani back to her, then perhaps seize the goddess away. We can't risk it. So she will be with me."

He'd given the whole situation far more thought than I'd given him credit for. Still, I would have felt more at ease with Tommy.

I think Tommy would have too, but he decided not to argue anymore. "Fine. Thirty minutes back at the restaurant."

Ling just smiled. He didn't seem to do that very much, and with the reflected street lights only half-illuminating his white teeth, it was pretty disconcerting.

I watched with more than a little trepidation as Tommy, my companion since this had begun, disappeared around a Shanghai corner and I was left alone with Ling Tau Meng.

"Come with me," he barked. Without waiting for a reply, he quickly marched deeper down the dark alleyway.

I hurried after him. "So where are we going?"

He didn't answer. I found that a little disturbing too.

"Where are we going?" I repeated, trying to sound firm.

"You have residual value," he answered. It didn't seem particularly responsive to my question.

"Come again?"

Ling stopped his quick march to turn and look back at me. I stumbled to avoid crashing into him.

"What did you say?" he demanded. I really missed Tommy at that point.

"I said, 'Come again?' It means, 'What did you just say?'"

He considered. In the dim alley, the only feature I could make out clearly was the glistening whites of his eyes. They weren't reassuring.

"You have residual value," he repeated as he began rushing down the alleyway again. "The goddess has not settled in another host. That means she is holding out for you. We may be able to use you to lure her back."

I didn't really like his choice of the words 'use' and 'lure.' I was about to tell him so, when he stopped abruptly at a dirty back door to some warehouse or business.

"We're here," he announced, opening the heavy door with a loud crack and a long creak. "Get in."

Then he grabbed me by the arm and shoved me inside, slamming the door behind me.

TWENTY-SEVEN27

I spun around in the total blackness and started banging on the dirty metal door.

"Li—!"

A hand covered my mouth, muffling both my initial yell at being shoved into the building and my subsequent scream at being grabbed from behind. I threw an elbow backward, but my assailant seemed to expect it and pulled me back, swept my feet out from under me, then fell to the icy cement floor with me, cushioning my fall and landing on top of me. My face was covered in fuzzy warm hair and I heard Gabriela's voice whisper in my ear.

"Silence."

She waited to see if I would comply. I did.

Then she added, "They will hear you."

But 'they'—whoever they were—already had. I heard low, urgent voices and hard footsteps fast approaching. Gabriela heard them too and yanked me off the filthy floor. I couldn't see anything in the complete darkness, but I let Gabriela pull me along by my wrist. She seemed to know where we were going and in a moment she pulled me down some crumbling cement steps to a dank landing below the door Ling had pushed me through.

The owners of the voices arrived and were whispering to each other in a language I didn't recognize. Gabriela didn't need to tell me to be quiet but she placed a hand over my mouth anyway. I didn't resist.

They opened the door a crack and called out into the alleyway. There wasn't much light from the alley but compared to the total darkness we were otherwise in, it was enough to make out two men in dark clothes, guns in their hands.

They closed the door again and I could hear their scuffling footsteps as they ran back to whatever area they had come from in whatever building we were in.

Once I thought it was safe to whisper, I reached up and pulled Gabriela's hand away. But before I could ask what the hell was going on, she gave the faintest "Psst" to silence me, then pulled me to my feet again. Feeling along the grimy wall with one hand, my other hand firmly in Gabriela's grasp, we slunk silently along the back of the room.

But to where? I wondered.

A few moments later my question started to be answered. There was light ahead, enough to make out stacks of crates and boxes. We sneaked up behind them and crouched low. Gabriela then stood up and peered over the top of the wall of crates. She tugged me to my feet and pointed, but I was too short to see over the crates like her. So I found a crevice between two boxes and peered through.

I couldn't see everything, just a thin slit of the scene, like looking at a painting through a pinhole. But I could see enough.

A tall older man with thick white hair and furtive hands stood facing a younger man with black hair and a great tailor. I couldn't see the younger man's face, but even if I could have I likely wouldn't have been looking at it because seated in a chair between them, motionless and blindfolded, was Kyle.

TWENTY-EIGHT28

I had enough presence of mind not to yell out 'Kyle!'

But I sure wanted to.

He was just sitting there, his head flopped back, a blindfold over his eyes, and his arms tied to the back of the chair. The two men were obviously discussing what to do with him. No one had to tell me who the older guy was. I knew it was Nakajima.

He was tossing a coin in the air like an old time gangster. It was like he knew he was being watched and wanted to look the part of bad guy.

I tapped Gabriela on the shoulder and shrugged, trying to convey a 'What do we do now?' sentiment. She shrugged back, which I took as 'I don't know either.'

Then we heard more footsteps and more people came running up to Nakajima. I couldn't see who though, because they stopped short of the pool of light cast from the single light bulb hanging from the ceiling. But whoever it was brought agitating news because Nakajima threw his coin on the ground. It ricocheted off the cement floor at an odd angle with a metallic clank.

Nakajima immediately began scanning for it and I was

reminded of my earlier story about the man who'd lost a quarter on Fourth Street. I suddenly thought Nakajima might flip a switch to turn on all the lights, maybe exposing us. As much as I wanted to see what would happen next, I didn't want to get caught too. And I wasn't all that sure I really did want to see what happened next if that was something bad—well, worse—to Kyle.

I tried to think it through. If Nakajima was here, either my mom was here too or she was somewhere nearby with someone watching her. Kyle was either being used to find out information about us or as bait. What had Ling said? I had 'residual value.' So I needed to find out a way to make Nakajima leave in a hurry—too much of a hurry to bother lugging Kyle along. And maybe too much of a hurry to go back and get my mom from whatever seedy hotel she was hidden away in.

A quick scan of the room gave me an idea. I looked around for something to throw. Two somethings actually. The first, something breakable and hopefully loud. The second, something smallish and heavy.

I silently slid the top off a small crate next to me. Gabriela grabbed my arm to stop me, but I shook it off. Inside were various vases and baubles, ready for overseas shipping. They would have to do. The vase was perfect, but the jade elephant was a little smaller than I'd have liked. Oh well.

I stood up and threw the vase as far as I could to the right side of the warehouse. When it hit the floor, the crash echoed off the walls and everyone, including Nakajima, rushed over to see what had happened. Then I stepped out between the crates and threw a perfect strike, nailing the jade elephant off the glass fire alarm box I'd seen on the opposite wall.

The warehouse filled with an earsplitting siren. Nakajima and his cronies were at the edge of the light, their faces hidden in shadow, but I could still make out their actions as first they hesitated, then motioned toward Kyle, then left him there and ran for the front exit.

Gabriela darted out from the other side of the crates and we ran over to Kyle. I yanked the blindfold off his face, revealing a shiny black eye. Gabriela went to untie his hands, then looked up at me in surprise.

"His hands aren't tied. They're just limp."

I shook Kyle but his head just flopped forward like a rag doll's.

"Oh my God!" I covered my mouth with my hands. "He's dead!"

TWENTY-NINE29

Gabriela grabbed his wrist and put an ear to his mouth.

"He's not dead," she almost sobbed. "In fact, his pulse and breathing are strong."

She bent down and scooped him up like a baby. I was stunned at her strength.

"Let's go," she whispered. "We are not safe yet."

"Okay," I was quick to agree. Then I remembered something. "Hold on." I darted into the half-light. I'd watched where that coin had bounced and decided to see if I could find it really quick. It might give us a clue about where Nakajima had been or where he might be next. Maybe it was a Russian ruble or a Mexican peso.

But it was a million times better than that. A billion times.

I scooped it up and shoved it into my pocket. Then I ran back to Gabriela. I gave her a thumbs up and we ran out onto the street, each carrying our own precious cargo.

THIRTY30

We were going to go back to the restaurant, hoping to run into Tommy, but even Gabriela's strength had its limits. After a couple of blocks she had to put Kyle down.

We tried to prop him up into a sitting position but he kept flopping over. Finally we just dragged him away from the street and leaned him against the building there.

I picked up a limp arm by the wrist and let it fall with a fleshy thud. That should have hurt but he didn't even flinch.

"Are you sure he's not dead?" I asked.

"He's definitely alive." She pulled open an eyelid to reveal a glistening but unfocused eye. "He's just unconscious."

I considered the possibilities. "Coma?"

Gabriela shook her head. "I wouldn't think so. Aside from his eye, he seems fine. It's like he's, he's—"

"Like he's asleep," I realized.

We looked at each other. "Hypnosis," we said in unison.

"So how do we snap him out of it?" I asked.

Gabriela shrugged. "I have no idea."

I snapped my fingers in front of his face. That usually

worked on TV. Not so much in Shanghai, though. He didn't wake up.

Gabriela tried two sharp claps in front of his face. Again, nothing.

We were stumped for several minutes. Then I had an idea.

I lifted his chin in my hand and lowered my voice. "Kyle Emerson, when I count to three and snap my fingers you will wake up. You will not remember anything that has happened. One... Two..."

"And you will fall madly in love with Gabriela Paiz!" she interjected.

I dropped Kyle's chin and glared at her. "What are you doing?"

She laughed. "I wanted to see if it would work."

"Don't cheat, Brazil. If he likes you, he likes you—and I think he does—but don't mess with his mind."

Gabriela's smile faded, but only a bit. "You are a good friend."

I muttered a "Thanks," at the same time she muttered, so I almost didn't hear her say, "May the best girl win."

I ignored it. I didn't even want in the game.

"Kyle Emerson," I tried again, "when I count to three and snap my fingers you will wake up. You will not remember anything that has happened. One... Two..."

"Excuse me," Gabriela interrupted again. "But do you think perhaps you should tell him that he *will* remember everything?"

I frowned at her. She had a point, damn it.

"Fine. Take three." I grabbed his chin again. "Kyle Emerson, when I count to three and snap my fingers you will wake up. You will remember everything that has happened. One... Two... Three!"

I snapped my fingers. Nothing happened, at first.

But after a few moments Kyle lifted his head from my hand and shook it slightly. Then he groaned and placed a palm against his bruised eye.

He opened the other eye and looked up at me and Gabriela. "Ow."

I crouched down next to him and touched his hair. "What happened, Kyle?"

"You ran away from me," Gabriela reminded him, also crouching down.

Kyle looked down for a moment, then his exposed eye widened and he looked at me. "I saw your mom, Jen! I saw her with two men, turning a corner. I— I had to go after her."

Then he looked down. "At least, I thought it was your mom. Maybe it wasn't—"

"No, Kyle, you were right. It was my mom."

"How do you know?"

I looked past him down the alley and stood up.

"I'll tell you later," I said. Then I turned to face the giant ghost dragon rushing at us.

THIRTY-ONE31

Gabriela saw the ghost dragon too. She rushed over and covered Kyle with her body. Nice. That left me standing against the wall as the white outlined monster roared and reared its horned head three stories high.

It spotted us—or me, it seemed—and darted its head right at me. I dove out of the way just in time and the dragon's snout smashed into the building. Any hope I might have had that a ghost wouldn't be able to touch me were easily dispelled by the brick and plaster that went flying all over when the apparition's head crashed into the wall.

I rolled into the alleyway and propped myself onto my hands and knees. The dragon spirit shook its head and looked around for me. It only took it a second to spot me and it raised its ghost head again a good twenty feet, looking down at me with black eyes. It roared—a haunting, otherworldly roar—then opened its fang-filled mouth and, I think, smiled. I didn't know a lot about dragons, but I knew the breathing fire thing. So I was pretty sure it was about to breathe ghost fire on me.

I wasn't sure what ghost fire would be like really, but I was pretty sure it would be bad. I hadn't ever been in that type of a position before—except the time the lunch lady walked up from behind and caught me making fun of her to the kids at my table—so I wasn't really prepared. I hadn't brought my magic ghost anti-dragon sword.

But I had something else. I looked down in my hand at the shiny bauble Nakajima had been tossing in the air.

It was a golden brooch in the shape of a flower. And not just any flower: the traditional 16-petaled chrysanthemum associated with the Japanese imperial throne. It had a dark blood-colored garnet at its center. And I'd seen it a hundred times in my mother's jewelry box.

I remembered what Tommy had done in Rio, so I held up my mother's totem just as the dragon unleashed its frozen ghost fire breath down on me.

The fire split apart when it hit the brooch and fell all around me, flying off the black pavement in white sparks and shoots. The pavement was seared, but I was safe. The brooch surrounded me in a bubble of protection. The dragon reared back and tried again. Twice as much fire came out of its mouth that time, but it was all deflected by the brooch. It was my umbrella in a ghost dragon fire breath rain storm.

The beast turned its head and looked at me with one dead eye. Then it lowered its head to the ground, ready to try again. I thought maybe this time it might just try to eat me. So I decided to beat it to the punch.

I jumped at the dragon's snout and pressed the brooch against the freezing cold, immaterial ghost flesh I found there. The dragon started to roar and I thought maybe I'd managed to hurt it. But it was even better. It began spinning, then twisted itself into a long knotted plume of smoke and disappeared, leaving the echo of its roar to fade away in the suddenly empty alley.

"What was that?" Kyle yelled at me.

"What did you do?" Gabriela asked.

"How are you still here?" Ling demanded as he stormed up the alley from the same direction the ghost dragon had appeared.

THIRTY-TWO32

I started backing up, my knees bent and my arms extended in a ready position. "Watch out, guys. He's the one who pushed me into that warehouse."

Before Kyle and Gabriela could do more than look up at the advancing Ling, he replied. "Of course I did." His tone was almost bored, definitely irritated.

"So, so, so you don't deny it?" I stammered.

Ling had reached our group, and I had stopped retreating, although I was still half crouching.

"Why would I deny leading you to your missing friend?"

I wasn't sure how to respond. That's not really how it had seemed to me at the time.

"But how could you have known—?" I started.

"Paiz isn't the only one with abilities," Ling gruffed. "I just don't go around flaunting them at every possible minute."

That seemed plausible. But I still wasn't completely convinced. "Why didn't you come in with me?"

He was ready with his answer. "I circled around to the front. By the time I got there the fire alarm was going off and Nakajima was running down the street."

"What about the dragon?" I demanded.

"What dragon?" I couldn't read Ling's expression on the dark street.

"The giant white ghost dragon you sent to attack us," I accused.

Ling narrowed his eyes and crossed his arms. "I sent no such beast. But if you've seen the Spirit of the Loong, this is very serious indeed. Nakajima must have recruited the Chinese destruction godling."

Gabriela looked up at me to see what I would say. I couldn't help think about the cryptic warning from the unknown girl on my flight. *Be careful whom you trust.*

"Let's find Tommy," I huffed. I tapped Kyle on the head, told him to get up and stormed past Ling, who was smiling again, damn him.

THIRTY-THREE33

Tommy was waiting at the rendezvous point, but I kept the explanation to a minimum. I wanted to get off the street as soon as possible. But I had a dilemma: I wanted to tell him about Ling, but it was Ling's apartment we were going to.

"What happened to your dragon?" Kyle asked Ling as he plopped down on one of the leather couches.

"What happened to your eye?" Tommy asked Kyle now that he could see the shiner in full light.

"What happened to my mother?!" I yelled. "That's what this is all about. Not spirits and godlings and dragons and spooky warehouses where people you thought were your friends shove you inside with strange men with guns!"

Everyone looked at me, apparently stunned by my outburst.

"That's what this is about," I repeated weakly. "Where is my mom?"

Kyle stood up and put a hand on my shoulder. "We'll find her, Jen. I promise. I heard them talking about leaving again soon."

I turned to look him in the face. "Did you hear where?"

Kyle shook his head. "No. But they're definitely collecting

totems. They said they had a few already. Gabriela's, Ling's, and your mom's."

"Not my mom's." I smiled and pulled out the brooch. "Not any more."

"Let me see that!" Ling tried to snatch it out my hand, but I was too quick for him.

I gave him one of his own smug smiles back. "Ah, ah, ah. Mine."

Then I turned to Gabriela. "Can you use it to see where they're going next?"

Gabriela frowned. "I don't think so. I could probably see where they are now, but I've never been able to see into the future."

I didn't bother asking Ling; he wasn't touching my totem.

"Tommy?" I asked.

Tommy had sat down across from Kyle. When Gabriela was explaining why she couldn't do it, he'd hung his head and dropped his hands between his knees. At the sound of my voice, he looked up. He smiled weakly, almost painfully.

"I might be able to help," he said. "But I don't think you want me to."

THIRTY-FOUR34

I couldn't believe it. "What do you mean I won't want you to do it? Of course I want you to find my mom. Have you been able to find her this whole time?"

Tommy just gave his usual calm smile. "No, Jeni. I haven't been able to find her this whole time. I'm not even sure I can do it now. I can try, but if I succeed, there will be a price."

That didn't sound good. "What kind of price?"

"We are all godlings, tethers for our spirits to stay connected to our world. But each of our spirits is different, just as we are different. Gabriela's spirit helps her see things she can't see, like a man standing on another man's shoulders to look over a distant hill. Her goddess does that willingly, happily. But mine ..."

He trailed off. I looked at Gabriela but she didn't look back at me. She was watching Tommy, her face twisted into an expression of sympathy and guilt. Kyle looked at me though, and raised his eyebrows as if to say, 'Can you believe all this?' Ling just leaned against his plaster-dusted cabinet, arms crossed and face locked in scowl mode.

Tommy seemed like he wasn't going to say any more, so I

prodded him. "What is it about your spirit? Why don't you want to help me?"

Tommy looked up sharply, hurt in his eyes. "Oh no, it's not that I don't want to help you. I do want to help you, Jeni. But if I help, I will also hurt."

"Can we stop the cryptic warnings, Tommy?" Kyle interrupted. "What are you trying to say?"

Tommy nodded. "My spirit will help, but he will exact a price. He is not at peace with his current lot. He feels disrespected and forgotten even by his own people—what are left of them. So he may tell me where your mother is, but I fear the price will be that we won't be able to do anything with our knowledge. He'll tell us, but then he'll make sure we never find her."

"Like Cassandra," said Kyle.

I looked at him. "Who?"

He rolled his eyes at me. "Do you ever read?"

I wasn't sure what to say. I didn't read nearly as many books as him.

"Cassandra was the daughter of Prium, King of Troy," Kyle explained. "Troy, as in Helen of Troy. Have you at least heard of her?"

"Yes," I sneered. "Of course."

"Okay, so Cassandra was so beautiful she was blessed by Apollo with the ability to see the future. But the blessing came with a curse: no one would ever believe her."

Well, Tommy sure was beautiful, I thought, but I considered the rest of Kyle's explanation. "So we're not going to believe Tommy?"

"Oh, you'll believe me," Tommy said. "It just won't matter."

I looked again at Kyle. "It's not a perfect analogy," I observed.

Kyle threw up his hands. "Sorry. At least I knew the story."

I handed Tommy the brooch. I noticed Ling pushed himself up from his leaning stance, eyes fixed on the piece of jewelry, but he didn't make any moves toward it.

"Tell me where my mother will go next," I instructed Tommy. "You said it yourself: we need to head them off. I bet your spirit won't do us wrong."

Tommy closed his hands around the golden chrysanthemum. "I'm not much of a gambler. I guess we'll just see."

He walked over to a carpet behind the couches and sat on the floor. He squeezed my brooch in one hand, and with the other he extracted his stone bear and clasped his hand around the statue. He began to chant in a strange language, low quiet words, rhythmic and urgent. As he said them, he nodded and swayed front to back.

I looked at Kyle to give him a 'Weird, huh?' look, but he was watching Tommy intently. So was Gabriela. I looked at Ling and he gave me the look I'd wanted to give Kyle. That made me angry and embarrassed, so I turned back to watch Tommy.

After a few more minutes, Tommy stopped the chanting, then the nodding, then the swaying. Then he opened his eyes. He didn't let go of the totems.

"I could see the city she'll go to next, but I couldn't recognize it."

"Well, so much for that!" Ling interjected. "We still need to eat dinner—"

"Hush!" Gabriela shot him a killer look. She turned back to Tommy. "Describe what you saw, Thomas."

Tommy closed his eyes to help retrieve the memory of the vision. "It was a city. A big, crowded city. A city on the water. And it was hot."

"Oh, that narrows it down to most of the cities in the world," sneered Ling.

"Did you see any landmarks?" Gabriela tried.

Tommy frowned. "A church, I think."

"Very helpful," Ling laughed. "Shall I book our tickets now? This is a waste of time. He obviously didn't see anything valuable."

Gabriela ignored him. "What did the people look like?"

Tommy thought for a moment, then nodded. "There were lots of different people, but most of them were African. It was in Africa. West Africa, I think."

Gabriela smiled. "Lagos. She's going to Lagos next."

"Lagos?" I asked. "Is that a place?"

"Wow," Kyle said, exasperated. "Do you own an atlas?"

"Hey, back off," I warned him. "I rescued you."

He had to smile at that. "Lagos is the capital of Nigeria," he explained.

"And home to Edo Adebalo," Gabriela said, "godling to Ngai, the West African god of creation."

THIRTY-FIVE35

It was too late to go to the airport, and besides we were all exhausted and famished. I felt bad not being out on the streets looking in every window crack for my mom, but Shanghai was a huge city and the last time I'd tried that I'd almost been caught by armed bad guys. Besides, now we knew where they were going next and would be able to head them off at the pass, so to speak.

I got to share a guest room with Gabriela. Well maybe 'got to' is too strong. More like I had to. Boys in one room, girls in the other. Actually, Ling in his room, girls in the spare room, and boys on the living room couches. Still, I was looking forward to lying down in a bed, even if I had to share it with a six foot tall Brazilian girl who was trying to steal my not-boyfriend.

I know. It was confusing to me too. I tried not to think about it and just get ready for bed. While Gabriela went down the hall to wash up, I grabbed my purse to see what, if any, toiletries I might have hidden in there. At least some breath mints, I hoped. I unzipped it and stuck my tired hand in, feeling around for a pack of gum or something.

Instead, my hand settled around a cell phone. Not mine—it

was too big to be mine. It was Tommy's; I recognized it from the trip to the airport. Staring at it, I wondered how it ended up in my purse. Then I remembered the girl from the plane: she had bent down and messed with our bags before she got up and left. Did she put it in there? If so, why? Would it show me that I couldn't trust Tommy either? Was he lying about the ritual not really working? Or maybe he was lying about Lagos completely. Maybe my mom was back in Seattle, wondering where her daughter was and why her house was burnt to the ground.

I didn't know whether I should turn on the phone and search the files and apps. I wanted to, but it was such an invasion of privacy, such a breach of trust. Then again, did he deserve my trust?

But my decision was avoided when Gabriela stomped back into the room.

"The bathroom is free," she chimed.

I dropped the phone back into the purse and zipped it shut. "Thanks. I'll go clean up."

I didn't tell her about the phone, but it weighed on my mind all night.

THIRTY-SIX36

Lagos was really, really hot. Apparently it's about three feet from the equator, so there's no real need for things like, say, clothes. We stepped out of the air-conditioned plane and were hit by a thick blanket of tropical hot.

The flight had been long and irritating. Kyle came with me of course. So that meant Gabriela came too. Ling had also insisted on coming, although I half-suspected it was because he believed Tommy when he said we'd fail, and he wanted to be there to see it.

Tommy sat next to me the whole way. Ordinarily I would have loved that, but right then it was irritating because it meant I couldn't look at his phone which was still in my purse. I tried not to seem suspicious of him, but I don't think he would have noticed anyway. His demeanor had changed ever since he'd done his ritual. Before that he had been calm and confident. Now he was still calm, but the confidence was gone. It wasn't that he was scared, but you could tell he didn't think we would succeed. I hoped his creation spirit would give us a chance.

The whole thing was making me wonder what my godling would be like. It hadn't occurred to me that they would have unique personalities. Would mine influence my personality? Had it influenced my mom's?

Then I remembered I was trying to rescue my mom, not gain goddess super powers. That made me feel guilty. So I was glad to focus on finding a taxi.

"Where are we going?" I asked Tommy, but he just shrugged.

"Edo lives downtown," said Gabriela. "We should go there first."

We found the line of taxis outside the airport, but they were all subcompacts. There was no way all five of us could fit in one. I wanted to suggest Ling stay at the airport, but before I could, the others decided we would split up: me, Kyle, and Gabriela in one car, Tommy and Ling in the other. We walked up to the first two taxis waiting and explained our plan. Gabriela wrote out Edo's address on a scrap of paper and gave it to our driver. He nodded and we all got in.

Our driver started the engine, then turned around to Gabriela. "Miss, could you go ask your friend in the other car if he will want both cars to wait while you call on your friend? I need to let my dispatcher know."

Gabriela frowned, but pulled herself out of the small car. "Okay, I'll be right back."

She managed to force her large body out of the small vehicle and walk back to Tommy and Ling's taxi. And it was just as she reached their car and leaned down to the car window that our driver slammed our car into drive and peeled away.

THIRTY-SEVEN37

"Oh my God!" I yelled as I was thrown back into the car's seat. "Where are we going?"

Kyle didn't seem to get what was happening. He leaned forward and tapped the driver on the shoulder. "Uh, excuse me, sir. You forgot our friend back there."

The driver, a young man with dark skin and bright eyes turned to smile broadly at Kyle then went back to looking where he was driving.

Kyle sat back again and shrugged. "I guess we'll just meet them at Edo's place."

I grabbed Kyle by the shirt. "We're being kidnapped."

He looked at me like I was speaking Greek. "Kidnapped? What makes you say that?"

"The driver sent Gabriela out of the car on a ruse and then sped away with us. You and me. The only ones not linked to a god."

Kyle looked at me, then at the driver, then back at me. "Are you sure?" he whispered.

I rolled my eyes. "Hey, driver, are you kidnapping us?" I called out.

This time he didn't turn around but I could hear the broad smile in his voice. "Yes, miss. I am."

I looked at Kyle wide-eyed and gestured at the driver. "See?"

Kyle pushed himself back in his seat, clearly shaken. "Well, this sucks."

I could hardly argue with that, but before I could agree either, the driver spoke up.

"Don't you two kids worry yourself. You're in no danger. It will all make sense when we get there."

I had a hopeful thought. "Is the other driver taking our friends to the same place?"

Our driver laughed. "Oh no, miss. Definitely not."

I wasn't sure what to make of that. I looked at Kyle but he was just slumped in his seat staring straight ahead. Looking out the window, I could see we were on some sort of highway, heading out of town. We were traveling way too fast to risk jumping out. Besides, for some reason—maybe our driver's friendly demeanor—I was more curious than scared.

I relaxed back into the seat and looked out my window. The countryside was lush and beautiful. I hoped our destination would prove to be just as nice.

THIRTY-EIGHT38

The car pulled off the highway and followed a bumpy dirt road for way too long. Kyle and I just looked at each other, wondering where we would end up, but not really wanting to speak in front of our driver, and not really knowing what to say anyway.

The car finally stopped in front of a small village of earthen huts. I expected our arrival to be a major event, but the few people I could see walking about ignored us and kept to their work. Mr. Driver opened my door first.

"Miss Tanaka," he gestured for me to exit the vehicle, "Edo will see you now."

"Edo?" Kyle repeated. "You took us to Edo? But I thought—"

"Do not think too much, Kyle Emerson," our driver interrupted. "Sometimes you must also feel."

I, meanwhile, was sitting in my seat, arms crossed, staring straight ahead.

"Miss Tanaka?" Driver prodded.

"I'm not going anywhere," I said without looking at him. "I don't meet with people who kidnap me."

Driver laughed. "A wise rule. And a foolish one. Perhaps you were kidnapped. Perhaps you were rescued. You must decide. Your host is in that hut in the middle there."

With that, he left the door ajar and walked away. I turned just enough to watch him out of the corner of my eye as he ducked into a small hut at the end of the row.

I looked at Kyle. He just shrugged.

"What do you think we should we do?" he asked.

I knew what made sense, but I was surprised by how I felt. What made sense was to figure out a way back to Lagos and find Tommy and the others. But what I felt was we should go into that hut and meet Edo.

"Come on." I grabbed his hand. "Let's go meet our rescuer."

THIRTY-NINE39

I had expected the hut to be more, well, hut-like. Outside it was all earthen walls and grass roof. Inside it was all fine carpets and rich furniture. Our host/kidnapper/rescuer sat in a beautifully carved wooden chair facing the door. He was reading some rather thick book and smoking a pipe. The whole hut smelled of sweet pipe smoke.

When we walked in he looked up and nodded in greeting, then went back to reading. We looked around for someplace to sit and settled on a small couch near the window. Kyle nudged me in the ribs with an elbow, but I turned and shrugged. Even a whisper would have felt like a shout in the silent room.

Finally the man picked up a bookmark and set the book aside. "My apologies," he smiled warmly. "I hate to stop reading in the middle of a chapter. Thank you for coming."

I actually laughed a little at that. "We didn't have much of a choice in the matter."

He smiled again. "You always have a choice, Miss Tanaka. But you do not always realize it."

"You kidnapped us away from our friends and drove us to the end of the Earth," I pointed out. "I'm not seeing a whole lot of choice there."

"I apologize if my methods were extreme, but I do not believe you would have come of your own accord. We have choices but we often choose wrongly."

Kyle shifted in his seat. "Are you Edo?"

The man smiled at Kyle. "Yes and no. I am Edo now but I will not be Edo later."

"What does that mean?" I demanded. "And why did you bring us here?"

"It means that when others ask you if I am Edo you will say yes, but when you ask yourselves that same question you will say no."

I looked at Kyle but he just raised an eyebrow in response.

"And the reason I had you brought here," Edo/Not-Edo went on, "was to gain information and to give information."

"What information do you want to gain?" I asked.

He smiled, the same broad warm smile the driver had shown when he confirmed he was kidnapping us. "I have already gained it. Now, let me give some."

He sat forward in his chair and took my hand. His were big and strong, but smooth. "If the chain is only as strong as its weakest link, then we are in grave danger because that link is shattered, and therefore the chain is worthless. But if the blacksmith makes a new link, with the best metal, and crafted in the most expert way, then the weakest link becomes the strongest and may bear the stress of the entire chain."

I waited for more, but apparently that was it. "That's a long way for a clichéd metaphor."

That made him laugh. A deep belly laugh. "Then let me offer

you more. A warning and a charge."

I didn't like the sound of 'warning' and I wasn't really sure what he meant by charge. But I didn't have time to think about it.

"Here is the warning: what seems to be is not, and what is not, is. Here is the charge: to be the iron that rebuilds the chain you must first find the ore."

I stared at him for a minute, expecting—or maybe just hoping— for more.

"Not real helpful," I finally said. "I'm not real good with the whole cryptic riddle thing."

Kyle spoke up. "I think all riddles are cryptic, Jeni. That's kind of the point."

"Again, not helpful," I said to Kyle. Then I turned back to the man potentially known as Edo. "Can you give me anything more concrete? Like maybe where my mom is, or where she might end up next?"

Our host's smile disappeared into an expression of serious thought. "You are focused on your true goal. That is good. It will serve you as you make your choices. Here is another choice: your mother is either is the midst of a city, or in the midst of desert. She is in a crowded metropolis, or a sparsely populated wasteland. She is one of millions, or the only one. Choose wisely."

This was really starting to bug me. I hadn't asked to be kidnapped. I hadn't asked to be rescued. I hadn't asked for riddles. I hadn't asked for any of this.

"How about you choose to be straightforward," I said, "and give me a real location?"

Edo-or-Not smiled and met my challenging gaze. "Mumbai or the Australian outback."

I'm not sure what surprised me more, the sudden clarity of the response, or the information itself. Before I could decide, he surprised me again.

"Now, Jeni Tanaka, before we part, you may ask me two questions." Again the broad grin. "Choose wisely."

FORTY40

"Will Seattle ever win the World Series?" Kyle blurted out.

I slammed a hand over his mouth. "Oh my God! Shut up, Kyle." I turned to Edo. "That doesn't count! Please say that doesn't count."

He smiled. "It doesn't count. The questions are yours, not his. Although..." But he let the thought trail off with just a smile.

I pulled my hand away from Kyle's face and scowled at him "Hush, you. I need to think."

I looked down and frowned in concentration. I had so many questions. I had big questions like, 'Is this even real?' and 'What is this all about?' and 'Why me?' I had small questions like, 'How do we get back to Lagos?' and 'Is Kyle going to start dating Gabriela?' and 'Why is Ling such a jerk?'

I knew what one of the questions would be, had to be. I decided to use the other question to help me solve a more personal dilemma.

"Should I look at it?" I asked, knowing Kyle wouldn't understand but our host would.

Edo/Not-Edo nodded. "Yes, but don't let him catch you."

That was kind of what I figured, but now I could go through Tommy's phone with a little bit clearer conscious.

Then the obvious question. "Will I find my mother?"

"Yes," he sighed. Then he shook his head. "But you should have said 'rescue.'"

His reply stuck a dagger in my heart. "Wait! I mean *rescue*! Will I *rescue* my mother?"

"Our time together is finished," Edo/Not-Edo announced, and he took his book back from the table, opening it where he'd left off. "You may leave now."

"Edo, please." I took his strong hand in my weak ones. "Please."

He sighed again and looked me in the eye. "There are two sides to every question and every problem. You asked your question and I answered it. Do not ask me what I meant by my answer. Instead, ask yourself what you meant by your question."

I just stared at him, trying to understand.

Kyle gently took my arm. "Come on, Jeni. Let's go."

But as I pulled away, I felt Edo press something into my hand. "A parting gift," he whispered. "It is not what it seems."

Then Kyle and I turned and stepped through the hut door. But instead of the hot day and the village and the car, we found ourselves alone in the air conditioned hallway of a steel and glass high-rise.

FORTY-ONE41

I looked up, down and all around. Then I looked at Kyle.

"We were in a hut just now, right?" I asked.

He nodded slowly. "Okay, good," he sighed. "I'm not crazy."

"Or else we both are," I replied.

I turned around and looked at the door we had just walked through. It looked just like all the other hallway doors, marked simply with its unit number: 2222. I thought about knocking but I knew it would go unanswered.

I looked down at Edo/Not-Edo's parting gift. It was an exact replica of my mother's brooch, except the stone was a brilliant emerald color.

"Is that your mother's brooch?" Kyle asked, craning his neck to see.

"Yes and no," I joked. Then I pushed it into my pocket with its fraternal twin. "I'll explain later."

We walked over to the hall window and looked down on Lagos from twenty two stories.

"What just happened?" Kyle asked as he took in the majestic view.

I shook my head. "I don't know. It's like we were in two places at once."

"Is that possible?" Kyle asked.

"None of this is possible, Kyle," I pushed my hands through my hair. "Come on, let's go find the others. They're probably worried sick."

Well, Ling wasn't worried, I knew that. But Gabriela probably was, at least about Kyle. And I hoped Tommy was too. About me.

We reached the ground floor and stepped out into the hot, sunny afternoon. We had appeared on the 22nd floor of Lagos Towers, a downtown high rise only a short taxi ride from the airport. The airport, where we'd been not-kidnapped, seemed like the logical place to start, even though I knew they might be long gone by then, and we'd have to hunt all around downtown Lagos looking for them before going to the police station to see if they'd reported us missing.

But no need. They were all still at the taxi queue when we walked up. They didn't see us at first, but then Kyle yelled out "Gabriela!" followed by something in Portuguese. She turned and saw him, then ran over and picked him off the ground in a Brazilian bear hug. She spun him around and set him down again. Yuck. All that was missing was the field of wildflowers.

When Tommy walked up next, I joked, "No hug and twirl from you?"

He shrugged. "Not really my thing. But I am glad to see you. What happened?"

"You are not going to believe this!" Kyle started and I realized we should have gotten our story straight on the ride over. "We got kidnapped, but not really, and the guy took us to Edo, well maybe it was—"

"Maybe it was just a *misunderstanding*," I interrupted.

Something told me not to tell the others that the person we'd met might, or might not, have been Edo. But Kyle had already mentioned the name 'Edo' so I had to come up with something. "Our driver probably thought Gabriela would just ride to Edo's with you two."

"You didn't go to Edo's," Ling asserted. He had slunk up behind Tommy without so much as an 'Are you okay?'

"Yes, we did," Kyle was so excited to tell the story. Too excited. He didn't understand the stakes. "And it's even crazier than that. First, we drove right out of—"

"The airport," I finished. "We drove right out of the airport and over to Edo's."

I looked Ling in the eye. "Did you go to Edo's?" I asked, then remembered to add, "too?"

He didn't answer, but his eyes tightened a notch.

"No," answered Tommy. "We decided we should try to find you."

I threw my arms wide open. "Well you found us! And we met with Edo. So now we can leave Lagos!"

Gabriela looked at me like I was crazy. Ling looked at me like I was lying. Tommy looked at me like it didn't matter either way.

"Where should we go?" asked Tommy.

"That's the crazy part!" Kyle was still too excited. He didn't get it. "Either India or Australia."

That stunned all of them for a second. "Those are pretty different," Tommy finally said.

"And pretty far apart," added Gabriela.

"Edo was pretty cryptic," Kyle said. "Everything was in twos. This or that, yin or yang. He wouldn't tell us which was the right place."

Tommy looked at Ling, who raised an eyebrow in reply. "That does sound like Edo," Ling admitted.

"So where do we go?" Tommy threw the question open to all of us.

I knew what I was going to suggest, but I wanted to see what the others would say first. Ling was the first to jump in.

"Australia makes the most sense. We should go there."

"Why does it make the most sense?" I tried to sound curious, not accusatory, but wasn't sure I'd succeeded.

Ling didn't seem quite ready for the question. "Uh, well, because it's closer to where we were in China. And um, culturally, you know, it's a British colony, or it was, and you're American, and so, er..."

He was rambling. Tommy started to cut him off, but I jumped in. "I think that makes a lot of sense, Ling."

His smug smile started to return. "You do?"

"Yes," I answered. "So why don't you go there and the rest of us will go to Mumbai."

The smile evaporated in the anger that filled his eyes. "That is not what I was suggesting!"

This time it was me who was smiling. "I do think we should split up though. If there are two possible places, and five of us, it doesn't make sense for us all to go to the same spot."

Before Tommy, or Gabriela, or especially Ling could argue, I turned to Kyle. "I'd like you to go to the Outback while I go to Mumbai."

Kyle looked surprised and a little hurt.

Then I lowered my voice. "You're the only one I can really trust."

The hurt gave way to understanding, and a little bit of pride.

"Oh. Of course, Jeni."

Then Gabriela did just what I thought she'd do. "I will go with Kyle," she announced.

"I'll go with Jeni," said Tommy.

Good, I thought, my heart beating a little faster.

Ling crossed his arms and looked at us.

"Where are you going, Ling?" I asked.

"Me?" he sneered. "I'm going home."

FORTY-TWO42

Good, I thought again, but apparently I was the only one who felt that way.

"No, Ling," said Gabriela. "We need your help. You can't leave us now. We are so close to finding Jeni's mother."

"I don't really care about Jeni's mother," Ling answered coldly. "I care about what Nakajima has planned."

Kyle piped in. "Aren't those kind of intertwined?"

At that point, Tommy took Ling by the arm and led him out of our earshot. We watched—of course—and I could see them having a pretty heated discussion. Tommy was making a lot of gestures, pointing into his own palm, and shaking a finger at Ling. Ling was just standing there, arms crossed, but when he spoke there was an unmistakable intensity to his face. I tried to hear what they were saying but could only make out snippets.

"... we had a deal ..." said Tommy at one point, and later "... stick with the plan ..."

At other points, Ling said "... this isn't working ..." and "... you're too naive ..."

Finally though, Tommy must have won him over. They

walked back and Tommy announced, "Ling's coming to Mumbai with me and Jeni."

Oh joy, I thought. Why couldn't Tommy have just kept his big mouth shut?

The teams having been decided, we headed back into the airport to make our respective flight arrangements. As we got closer to the main ticketing concourse, I pretended I needed to tie my shoe. "You go on ahead," I called to the others. "I'll catch up."

They only hesitated for a second before continuing to walk, then I whispered, "Kyle!"

He turned and looked at me. I motioned for him to come back to me. He looked a little puzzled, but shrugged and crouched down next to me.

"Aren't you a little old to have me tie your shoe for you?" he joked.

I reached into my pocket and pulled out my mother's brooch. The real one. I made sure the others weren't looking, then pressed the brooch into Kyle's hand. "Here. Take this."

Kyle looked down at his hand. "Shouldn't you keep this? It's your totem, right?"

I shook my head. "You're not going to find my mom in Australia. I'm not sure how I know that, but I do. The bad guys want this and they think I have it, so it's safer with you. But only if you don't tell anyone you have it."

Kyle shrugged, "Okay, Jen. Sure."

"Anyone," I repeated.

"Anyone," echoed Kyle. "Got it."

"Not even Gabriela," I finally pointed out.

He raised his eyebrows. "Oh." He frowned. "But—"

I squeezed our hands still holding the brooch together. "Promise me, Kyle. Don't tell her. Not yet. Not till this is all over."

He hesitated, but then looked down. "Okay, Jeni. I promise. But I don't like it."

I smiled. "You're a good friend, Kyle. Thank you."

Kyle shrugged again. "Whatever." He slipped the brooch into his pocket. "Let's catch up to them."

I stood up and we hurried after the others. I was glad Kyle had made me the promise, but I knew he'd break it. In fact, I was counting on it.

FORTY-THREE43

I hadn't just chosen Mumbai on a whim. I may not have read as much as Kyle Smartypants, but I had to do school reports too. I knew Mumbai was the second largest city in the world, by population. Number two. Right behind Shanghai. I knew Edo was trying to communicate something to me with all the "two" this and "double" that. So Mumbai made the most sense.

But fourteen million people in one city feels a lot different when you know one of them and he has a nice apartment and a car to get you there and a great restaurant right around the corner. Fourteen million people and you don't know a soul can be pretty overwhelming. The first order of business was finding a hotel. Next would be to track down the godling to Brahma, the Hindu god of creation. But it was late. That would have to wait until morning.

As we piled into the taxi in the still hot Indian twilight, Ling told the driver, "Luxor Hotel. 32 Regency Street."

"You know a hotel here?" I asked, trying to make conversation. It had been pretty quiet without Kyle and Gabriela. I didn't like Ling much, but the lack of conversation was making me edgy.

"I know hotels in many places." He was as brusque as ever. Then, noticing Tommy's disapproving glance, he added almost amicably, "I travel a lot."

I looked out the window as I said, "I'm sure it's very nice."

I didn't say another word until we got there.

The hotel was just off the main street in Mumbai, near the financial district. It was, in fact, very nice. I was kind of glad, given some of the seedier areas we had driven through on our way from the airport. I supposed every city, even Seattle, had areas of disrepair and poverty, but it had been more jarring to see those same things in another country and culture. Still, the five-star tourist hotel helped me forget some of the destitution I'd seen on the city's outskirts.

Ling went to check us in. Tommy and I hung back in the lobby.

It was nice to be alone with Tommy, even for just a few moments, but I suddenly felt awkward and wasn't sure what to say. He didn't say anything either but it was different. He just smiled at me. And that was enough.

Then Ling walked up.

"They only had two rooms left." He handed me a key. "Your room is on the second floor. Tommy and I will share a room on the third floor."

I didn't really like the sound of that. I didn't want to be so far away from them or at least that far away from Tommy. Ling must have seen my expression.

"I figured you would want your own room," he explained. "Americans are modest like that, aren't they?"

I didn't like being stereotyped, but he was kind of right. I didn't want to share a room with two boys. But I didn't want to be alone either. I hadn't really been alone since this whole thing started.

Then I remembered Tommy's phone and Edo's approval of looking at it. I would need privacy for that.

"Okay. Great," I said, squeezing the key. "Yep. A girl needs her privacy."

"Good," said Ling with that mirthless smile of his. "Let's check out our rooms then meet in the lobby in ten minutes. I know a great Chinese restaurant just a few blocks away."

An hour later my stomach was full of orange chicken and rice and Tommy dropped me off at my room.

"Night, Jeni," he said simply. But there was something in his voice. Something I liked. I felt like he was dropping me off after a date. A date with some jerk from Shanghai who'd eaten all the spring rolls.

"Night, Tommy." I tried to sound cool, but not cold. Inviting, but not desperate. I wasn't sure if I'd done it though.

He walked down the hallway, and I closed and locked the door. Then I went straight to my purse, pulled out his phone and betrayed whatever trust he might have had in me.

FORTY-FOUR₄₄

Of course, trust is a two way street. And any trust I had for him was about to be tested too. I pressed the phone's 'ON' button and waited for the welcome screen to pop up. A few moments later the screen was filled with a picture of the big dipper. Ursa Major. The Great Bear.

Figured, I thought.

There were only a few icons on the desktop: 'Glitter,' an MP3 player, and, of course, Angry Birds. I clicked on Glitter.

The godling social media app opened up, but it took me to a login screen where I needed to enter both a username and a password, neither of which I knew. I made a few guesses ("TommyBluehorse," "Bluehorse," "TBHorse29") but got nowhere.

I went back to the desktop and pressed the menu button for more apps. Maybe there would be something buried deeper. I scrolled though the list.

Alarm clock. Camera. Calculator. Gallery. Izamani.

I stopped. Izamani no Mikoto. The Japanese creation goddess. The one who had tried to bond with me. The one who started all this. I tapped the icon.

It opened into a basic note program. There were several files I could select: Plans, Goals, Candidates, and the one I tapped on: Jeni.

It opened into a text page and I was greeted with a disturbingly accurate list of my personal data. Full name, date of birth, height, weight, eye color. Everything but the booking photo. There was even a summary of Tommy's thoughts and observations. Apparently Tommy had been watching me since long before he showed up on my back porch.

Jennifer Tanaka may be the ideal candidate for a godling. She appears to be unaware of the situation or her role in it. As such she may be open to manipulation/guidance regarding use of the connection.

'Manipulation'? I didn't like the sound of that.

The key will be whether the transfer is successful. If it is, the opportunity for influence may be lost. On the other hand an apparent failure may prove to be the ultimate success. Our efforts need to be focused on this event.

Did he *want* the transfer to fail? How could he have known I would reject the goddess?

If she joins our ranks, she may become a valuable tool.

Now I was a 'tool'? I was not liking the tone of this.

And not just because she's so pretty.

Then again...

But I didn't get to read any more because just then there was a noise at my door. I turned and saw that it was more than just a noise. Someone was turning the doorknob, trying to get in.

FORTY-FIVE45

I dropped the phone and crouched down on the floor behind the bed. I thought I'd locked the door, but it only took a minute for the knob to turn all the way and the door start to open, ever so slowly. So maybe I hadn't remembered to lock the door after all—or else my visitor had a key. Didn't the front desk of a hotel usually give you two keys? Ling checked us in...

I wasn't waiting to find out who it was. The stealthy entry broadcast ill intentions. A desire to catch me by surprise. But I wasn't about to be caught at all. I threw open the window next to the bed and scrambled through it even as my attacker inched the door open wider.

We were only on the second floor, so hanging onto the sill with both hands and lowering my feet down as far as possible, I was only a few feet off the ground. I let go and tumbled to the ground, my ankles stinging a bit, but my burglar left without his quarry.

I looked around. I was in the alley behind the hotel. Garbage bags were piled up against the wall, and the road was slick with some type—or types—of liquids. It wouldn't take my visitor long to figure out which way I'd gone, so I turned and ran up the alley, away from the hotel, away from Tommy and Ling, and into the dark Mumbai night.

FORTY-SIX46

It took me about two blocks to realize that maybe this wasn't such a good idea after all. Mumbai was very busy at night, but busy in a very tough, scary, 'oh that's right, I'm a fourteen-year-old American girl really far from home' kind of way.

The worst part about realizing I was horrendously out of place and frightened about it, was that everyone else around me could see it too. I froze in the middle of the street, looking around, trying to figure out which way to go. I was a perfect target.

A group of four kids started walking up to me. Three boys and a girl. They were probably only a few years older than me, but they looked like they lived on the street and had a way tougher life than I'd ever even heard of. One of the boys barked something at me in Hindi, but of course I didn't understand. Then the girl said something mean-sounding and they all started laughing at me. She reminded me of Chelsea.

I backed away from them, but tripped on the curb and stumbled against the wall behind me. By the time I regained my balance and turned to face them again, they were right on top of me. The girl grabbed me by the throat and the barker reached out and touched my hair, saying something I'm sure was rude.

I reared up and kicked the girl as hard as I could in stomach. It wasn't capoeira, but it hurt, and she fell back holding her stomach and screaming. The boys were stunned for a second—but only a second. Then they were angry. Barking-hair-stroker grabbed me by the neck and shoved me to the ground. I didn't really wonder whether he would hit a girl; I just wondered how bad it was going to hurt.

He pulled his fist back and bent down to punch me in the face. I covered up with my arms and waited for the blow to strike the side of my head.

But it never came.

Instead I heard a rush of wind, a thick, wet thud, and then screaming as my pack of attackers fled. When I looked up, I saw the barker/stroker/puncher crumpled on the ground at least fifteen feet away. I couldn't see where he was hurt, but a pool of thick, dark blood was spilling out from under him.

I stood up and looked around, trying to figure out what had happened.

"Tommy?" Maybe he'd followed me, I thought. "Ling?"

They didn't answer, but I did get a response.

From the shadows stepped three figures. A true pack. A pack of yellow-skinned, red-eyed, sharp-fanged demons.

I ran, even though I knew it wouldn't do any good.

FORTY-SEVEN47

I was surprised I even made it to the corner.

They tackled me from behind and pinned me to the ground. I knew I was going to die. I couldn't believe I was going to die in a Mumbai alley, murdered by demon-monsters. They rolled me over, with two of them holding my wrists out to the side while the third sat on my chest. I closed my eyes against their hideous faces and against what was coming. I hoped it would be quick.

But instead of a slash to my face, or teeth in my throat, they forced my hands open then tore through my pockets. When they didn't find anything, they began to snort and hiss. The one on top of me—the leader I supposed—grabbed me by the throat and shoved his horrible, foul-smelling snout in my face. His eyes held the question his monstrous mouth apparently couldn't form.

'Where is the brooch?'

Thank you, Kyle Emerson, I thought.

I didn't say anything. I didn't know what they were going to do, but at least they weren't going to get the brooch.

The leader's face turned from puzzled to enraged and I watched his brow crush angrily down onto his eyes, even as his paw began to crush angrily around my windpipe. I wondered who Izamani would find after I was dead.

"*Usase dura ho ja'o!*"

A girl about my age ran from nowhere and kicked the leader-demon in the head with a flying kick. The demon didn't let go of me, but it did stop squeezing. It watched as the girl kept moving past it, rolling on the ground and popping back up onto her feet in a ready fighting position.

The demon finally let go, but only to stand up and face my would-be rescuer. She circled back and motioned for me to get behind her. I scurried away from the demon and ran to her side, rubbing my sore throat.

"Thanks," I rasped.

"Do not thank me yet, Jeni," was her reply. "We are not out of danger yet."

That was an understatement. Two teenage girls against three fully grown demon-monsters.

"Be ready to run," she whispered. I was already ready.

She reached into her pocket and threw something breakable onto the ground. A thick red smoke poured out from the spot and filled the alley.

"Run!" She grabbed my arm and pulled me—but not away. She yanked us *toward* the monsters. In a moment, though, it all made sense as I felt them rush past us at where we had been. Now we were behind them, with them chasing in the wrong direction, thinking we had just turned and run away.

Rescuer-girl pulled me through the dimly lit, sticky streets. We turned at corner after corner, ducking through low passageways I didn't even see until we were in them. I didn't know if the monster-men would find us, but I knew for sure I was totally lost.

Finally, she stopped at a low doorway and pulled me inside.

I looked up and around. We were inside a temple.

She tossed back her hood and extended a hand in greeting.

"Jeni Tanaka. I am Samara, godling to Brahma. I have been waiting for you."

FORTY-EIGHT48

"Uh, pleased to meet you." I shook her hand awkwardly. "And thanks for saving me from those, those things."

She slipped her robe off and hung it in the wall. "My pleasure. And responsibility."

I cocked my head at that.

"A happy responsibility, to be sure," she clarified. "We godlings watch out for each other."

I rubbed the back of my neck. "Yeah, I'm not quite a godling yet. I kinda messed that up."

Samara put her hands on her hips. "Well, things happen in strange ways. I would not worry too much about it. Our bigger worry is Nakajima."

I nodded. "I know. We've been chasing him all over the earth. He's collecting artifacts for some sort of ritual."

This time it was Samara who cocked her head. "He has your mother, I believe?"

I felt a rush of shame that I needed to be reminded of my mother. I'd let the godling mission take precedence in my thoughts.

"He has brought your mother here," Samara went on. "That

is how I knew to find you."

"Well, I'm glad you did. What were those things?"

Samara frowned. "Most likely they were *rakshasas*. Regular people temporarily infused with evil spirits. It makes them inhumanly strong, but it also makes them subservient to whoever created them. So the question is—"

"Who created them?" I finished. "Nakajima, I would guess."

Samara nodded. "That does seem logical. But it's not really his style. Or his specialty. It's more of an Indian thing."

I supposed that made sense. "So maybe he's working with your counterpart, the godling to the Hindu god of destruction.

"Maybe," Samara considered. "Or maybe he's able to do things now which he wasn't able to do when there was proper balance."

And again it was my fault. I should have known it would come back to that eventually.

Samara seemed to sense the drop in my mood. "Come," she said. "Let's go into my quarters in the back of the temple. I have something for you."

As we walked into the main sanctuary, I tried out another theory. "What if it's not the balance? What if it's the totems that let him do new things?"

We reached the inner temple and Samara led me to a door in the back. "Which totems does he have already?"

I had to think about it for a second. "He has the Brazilian— or Candomblé—and the Chinese. He had the Japanese totem for a bit but I got it back."

"You did?!" Samara was about to open the door, but when she heard what I'd said, she spun back around. "Let me see it!"

She was a bit too eager and I realized I didn't know her from Adam. Or Eve, for that matter. I remembered the mysterious woman on the plane and Edo/Not-Edo's enigmatic warnings. But most of all I remembered that I'd given the brooch to Kyle, and I was very, very glad for it.

"I left it back at the room," I lied.

Her eyes flashed. "That was stupid! You can't leave it alone. This is too important."

I was starting to have second thoughts about this Samara person. She had seemed nice enough when she saved me from the monster-men. Now she was acting like Ling.

She caught herself. Shaking her head, she said, "I'm sorry. I didn't mean to yell. It's just, well, I just hope you understand how important these totems are."

"I do." That much was true. I wanted to tell her I'd actually given it to Kyle exactly because I understood. But instead I just repeated, "I really do."

Samara smiled. "Good," she said, opening the door. "Then come inside and prepare for your next task."

I followed her into the small office/apartment. It was jammed with furniture and books and pictures and sculptures and junk of every kind. If her totem was in there, it was perfectly hidden among all the other clutter.

She walked over to a bookshelf and slid aside a vase filling up one small shelf. She reached behind it and pulled out a sculpture of a four-armed man with an elephant's head.

She turned and held it out to me. "This is Ganesha, which is appropriate, for what we share is a gift."

"Uh, okay." I had no idea what she meant.

"I want you to protect my totem," Samara continued. "They are here to steal it. They will not suspect you have it. You must promise not to tell anyone."

I took the statuette. "I promise."

"Anyone," Samara repeated. I grinned as I recalled having the same conversation with Kyle.

"Anyone," I agreed. "Got it."

She reached into the shelf again. "Good. The balance is way off. It is now thirteen to ten. We cannot win out in the open. So we will win from our hiding places."

Then she pulled her hand out from the cubby hole of the bookshelf and threw a handful of sweet-smelling dust in my face. "You will be our last hope, Jeni Tanaka. Now sleep and honor your promise to me."

The last thing I remember before passing out was wondering if there was a pillow on the floor that was rushing toward me.

FORTY-NINE49

I woke up on top of the bed in my hotel room. My head felt thick and paper-thin at the same time. I didn't feel nauseous but I didn't want to sit up either. I just opened my eyes and tried to figure out where I was and how I'd gotten there.

"Was that a dream?" I murmured to myself. But then I felt the weight of an object in my left hand. When I lifted it to my face I saw it was Samara's elephant statue. Her totem.

"Nope. Not a dream."

I forced myself into a sitting position, then rested my head in my other hand. I actually felt kinda like I did after the goddess attacked me on my back porch, only less so. I just needed a minute to gather myself. I wondered if the hotel had lemonade.

Then there was a knock on my door.

What time is it? I wondered. The clock on the bedside table said 7:14. It was morning already? I felt like I hadn't slept at all.

Knock, knock, knock.

"Uhn..." I had trouble speaking at first. "Wh— Who is it?"

"Tommy," came his muffled voice through the door. "Can I come in?"

There was more to that question than met the ear. I was awake enough to know that. But I couldn't quite remember why. There was something I didn't want him to see. What was it again?

I looked down at my hands.

Oh right, I thought. *Elephant totem thing.*

I looked around for a place to stash it. The bedside table had a drawer. Maybe not the best place, but definitely the closest.

"Jeni?" Tommy called through the door. "Are you all right?"

"Yeah," I called out as I shoved the four-armed elephant-headed man totem into the drawer. "Coming."

I stumbled to the door. It was unlocked. I knew there was a reason why, but I was having trouble remembering all the details of the previous night. Especially stuff before the man-monsters attacked.

I swung the door open and stood there for a second.

Tommy looked me up and down. "You look terrible."

"Wow, Tommy Bluehorse. You sure know how to sweet-talk a girl." I turned and plopped down on the end of the bed.

When I did, I heard—we both heard—a small flop. The sound of something small on the bed being thrown up by the force of my sitting down, then falling again onto the sheets. And my heart sank as I suddenly remembered another detail from last night. We both looked. We both saw it. Tommy's phone.

We looked at each other, and then at the exact same time we both shouted, "I can explain!"

FIFTY50

"I didn't—" I said, just as he said, "The thing is—"

Then I said, "Well, okay, you see—" while he said, "It's not what—"

"I only—" I started.

"I didn't mean—" he said.

Then we stopped and looked at each other for a second. I started to move toward the phone, but Tommy was quicker. He snatched it off the bed.

"It was in my purse," I finally said. He was clearly flustered too, which calmed me down somehow. "I don't know how it got there."

He checked to see if it was on. It wasn't. Which was strange because I hadn't taken the time to turn it off.

"When did you find it?" he asked carefully as he pressed the 'ON' button.

A chirpy beep confirmed the battery was in fact not dead. That's when I remembered that someone else had been in my room last night—someone who'd tried to sneak in without my noticing. Maybe it wasn't to attack me, maybe it was to get Tommy's phone.

"I took it out last night," I sort of answered. "I was going to give it to you this morning."

He frowned and pressed the screen a few times.

"What are you doing?" I was afraid he'd be able to tell I'd opened some files.

He tapped the screen a couple more times. Then he visibly relaxed and looked up with a half smile. "Just making sure all the data is still there. It is."

He slipped the phone into his pants pocket. "I wonder how it got in your purse."

"Well, on the plane to Shanghai—" I started to tell him about the mysterious girl who'd sat next to me and jostled our bags. But then I heard Not-Edo's voice. 'Don't tell him.'

"Yes?" Tommy prompted.

"Oh, I was just going to say," I tried to think of something quick. "We were all pretty tired. You probably set it in there by accident or something."

That was lame.

Tommy thought so too. I could tell by the raised eyebrow. But he shrugged. "Okay. Well, at least I have it back now."

Then he looked at me again. His face repeated his earlier sentiment even if he was too polite to say it again. I looked terrible.

"Did you sleep in your clothes?" he asked.

I looked down. My shirt was wrinkled and my socks were half off. I suspected I had sheet creases on my face and I didn't even want to think about what my hair looked like.

"Uh, yeah." I suddenly wondered whether the demon-monster things had left any scratches on my face, or neck, or arms. "I'll just clean up really quick."

I hurried past him into the small bathroom attached to the room. I slammed the door shut and locked it.

"Um, Ling's meeting us in the lobby for breakfast," he called through the door. "Do you want me to wait for y—"

"No, no! Go on!" I called back as I examined the three fingernail scratches low on the left side of my neck. "I'll be down in just a minute."

Tommy didn't say anything for a few seconds. Then, "It'll be at least ten minutes, won't it?"

"More like fifteen," I answered, wondering if I had enough make up in my purse to cover up the scratches. "Probably twenty."

"Okay, great," Tommy said. "Ling will be thrilled."

"He'll be happy you got your phone back," I tried as I pulled my hair back and found another scratch behind my ear.

"Ling's never happy about anything," Tommy answered.

I thought he'd left and began scrubbing the dirt and dried blood off my skin, mumbling to myself about the predicament I found myself in, wondering whether I could pass them off as a rash or hives or something.

So when Tommy spoke through the door again, it startled me so much I let out a little scream.

"Let's not tell Ling about the phone just yet, okay?"

FIFTY-ONE51

By the time I got down to the lobby Ling and Tommy had already left and come back with breakfast.

"I wasn't going to wait twenty minutes for breakfast," Ling explained. He handed me a paper sack with a grease stain in the bottom corner. "Here."

I took it and looked inside. It was a delicious looking pastry that smelled of sugar and apples. "Uh, thanks. Sorry I took so long."

I really hoped that between make up, an upturned collar, and pulled-forward hair, I'd been able to conceal the scratches. I had my purse—with Samara's totem inside—slung over my shoulder. A promise is a promise. And I already knew the room wasn't safe.

"So what's the plan for today?" I asked Ling. Not sure why I didn't ask Tommy, but he was just standing there, looking at me all funny.

"We have big plans today," Ling answered with that smile. Maybe it wasn't as cold as it looked. Maybe it was just how he smiled. Still, I didn't like it. "We're going to meet with the Hindu godling of creation, to see if we can learn anything about Nakajima's plans."

"And your mother's whereabouts," Tommy added hastily.

Wow, I thought. I hadn't expected a reunion with Samara so quick. I was glad I'd brought her totem with me, so she'd know I took her charge seriously. On the other hand, I might ask her why she threw that dust in my face, and why she couldn't just have given me the totem this morning.

I pulled out the pastry and took a big bite. I was hungrier than I'd realized.

"Sounds great," I mumbled through the food. "Lead the way."

They did. The way led to the street, then to hailing a taxi, then down several unnamed streets until we reached a building that looked like it was either a temple, a school, a library, or a casino. I was surprised it didn't look nicer, given how splendid the inside had seemed when Samara and I had ducked into it from the back alley the previous night.

We hopped out of the taxi and walked up the cement steps. Tommy opened the door and I walked in behind Ling. The inside was definitely dingier than I remembered. Maybe that sleeping dust was messing with my memory, making everything look shiny and gold like when the goddess had tried to enter me.

Ling led us to a small doorway through which I could see a brightly lit and decorated room.

This must be what I remember, I thought.

Ling motioned for me to walk through. I did, as he called out, "Allow me to introduce the godling to Brahma, Hindu god of creation, Rajiv Bhatnagar."

A heavy-set Indian boy, maybe eighteen or nineteen years old, stood up from his throne-like chair at the back of the room.

"Welcome, Jeni Tanaka. Brahma has been waiting for you."

FIFTY-TWO52

"You can't be the godling to Brahma," I blurted out. "I already met her last night."

"Already met?" asked Ling.

"Last night?" asked Tommy.

"Her," said Rajiv. A rueful smile crossed his face, even as Ling and Tommy exchanged glances. "I see you have met my counterpart. Samara Kapur, godling to Kali, god of destruction."

I put my hands on my hips. "She said she was the godling to Brahma."

"Of course she did," Rajiv said. "She is a trickster. Our spirit of destruction is also our spirit of deception. For deception destroys."

I was unsure. I looked at Tommy and Ling. Ling was just standing there, arms crossed, with a sour expression hanging from his face. Tommy on the other hand had his arms extended toward Rajiv and was nodding, as if to say, 'He's the real one.'

"She saved me from some sort of man-monster demon things." I insisted.

Rajiv smiled. "Did she tell you who has the power to create

such beasts?"

"She said they would obey whoever created them."

Rajiv smiled broadly and tipped his head in agreement. His eyebrows raised to see if I got it. I did.

"Which is why they didn't really hurt me," I realized. "And why she was right there to stop them with nothing more than a kick. And why we were able to get away so quickly."

"You are a smart one," Rajiv grinned as he nodded. "She was unwise to try to fool you."

I slipped off my purse. "She gave me this." I pulled out the elephant-dude statue. I hated being tricked. "She said it was her totem and for me to guard it."

Rajiv's eyes widened, and I could see Ling react too, dropping his arms and craning his neck to see it. Tommy glanced at it, but returned his gaze to Rajiv.

"It is a totem," Rajiv said, "but not in the way she explained to you. Do you recognize the deity?"

I didn't even recognize that word. "The what?"

"The deity," Rajiv repeated. "You are not familiar with our gods?"

I shrugged, embarrassed. "I'm afraid not."

Rajiv nodded, as if he'd expected the American girl to be ignorant of his culture. "Then let me tell you that is a statue of Alakshmi, god of misfortune. She wanted you to carry it so misfortune would follow you."

I looked down at the statue in my hand, my blood beginning to boil at being fooled. I lifted it over my head, about to throw it to the ground.

"No!" shouted Ling and Rajiv at the same time.

I stopped myself. Ling looked to Rajiv, who looked at me. "That will only ensure even more misfortune," he exhaled. He put out his hand. "No, give the totem to me and I will take care of it properly."

I handed it to him with relief. I was angry too and a little disappointed. I had liked Samara. But I guess that was part of the deception too.

Tommy stepped next to me. He looked at Rajiv. "Nakajima is trying to steal all of our totems. If he was working with Samara, that confirms he is here in Mumbai. He will come for your totem next."

Rajiv stood up. "Never fear. My totem is safely locked away here in the temple."

"What is it?" I asked. I was genuinely curious. "A statue too?"

Rajiv smiled. "The less you know, the better." Then he frowned in thought. "But that gives me an idea. Nakajima wants all the totems. He was able to steal Ling and Gabriela's because they didn't expect him. But now we know he's coming and we can protect ourselves. He will not get my totem, but he has shown that he will not hesitate to attack you. Those demons searched you for your totem but did not find it. Next time, the next monsters may."

He extended a thick, strong hand. "Give me your brooch, Jeni. And I will keep it safe from Nakajima."

I looked to Tommy. He nodded encouragingly. I looked to Ling. He jerked his head impatiently at Rajiv.

I rubbed the back of my neck as I considered Kyle, and my totem, thousands of miles away in the Australian Outback. "Um, yeah. About that..."

FIFTY-THREE53

"I— I—" I couldn't figure out what to say. Something was keeping me from telling them the truth.

"Yes?" encouraged Rajiv.

"Spit it out," hissed Ling.

Tommy didn't say anything. He just looked at me with those big brown eyes of his.

"I'm not sure where it is," I finally said. "I think I may have lost it last night. During the attack."

"But the monsters didn't get it from you," Rajiv protested.

"I know," I threw my hands up, maybe a bit too exaggerated. "Crazy, huh? I must have dropped it just before that. Maybe when I was running, or dropping out the window."

"You dropped out of the window?" Tommy asked.

There was so much I hadn't had time to tell him. "Yes, someone was sneaking into my room. I didn't know who and I got scared so I snuck out the window and dropped to the first floor. I must have dropped the brooch then."

It was a terrible lie, but they seemed to be buying it. Well, maybe not Tommy, but the other two. Tommy raised an eyebrow at me, but I figured as long as he wasn't telling Ling about me having his phone, then he was probably okay with keeping his mouth shut about this too.

"This is very unfortunate," Rajiv said.

"This is unacceptable," Ling practically shouted. "If Nakajima got that brooch—"

"He doesn't have the brooch," I interrupted.

"How do you know?" He spat.

This time Tommy responded. "He doesn't have the brooch, Ling. Lower your voice."

It was time to change the subject. "So where's my mom?" I demanded of Rajiv.

He seemed taken aback by the request. "Uh... Where do you think she is?"

Classic avoidance. "Don't you have special powers or something to know?"

Rajiv laughed. "No. I am just a godling. I have powers and strengths and skills. But knowing your mother's whereabouts is not one of them."

I threw up my hands and turned to Tommy. "Then why are we here?"

Tommy opened his mouth to reply, but Ling spoke first. "Have some respect, girl."

"You could show me a little respect, Ling!" I barked. This was getting to be too much.

"You?" Ling laughed. "We are godlings. You are nothing."

I was trying to control my temper. I knew Ling could tell.

"No," he scoffed. "You are worse than nothing. You are a— what is the word?—a wannabe. A pathetic wannabe."

That did it.

"Shut up, Ling!" I yelled and ran toward him.

He took a defensive position, but held it casually, almost smugly. He clearly knew I wasn't a threat. And as I closed in on him I realized I wasn't a threat either, so I tried the one thing I could remember seeing Kyle do. I dropped to my hands and swung my leg out in a broad sweep at his legs.

No one expected me to do that, least of all Ling, and he wasn't ready for it. I knocked his feet out from under him and he stumbled backwards, finally falling on his butt.

Tommy laughed out loud and I could see Rajiv holding his laughter back. I even giggled a bit at my unexpected success. I wasn't mad anymore.

But Ling was. He was furious. He popped to his feet and started to come at me. I was helpless laying on the floor, my one lucky shot already spent. Thankfully, Tommy came to my rescue.

Before I could even see him move, he had crossed the distance to Ling, sailing over me and locking Ling's striking arm in his own. He tipped Ling off balance and tightened his grip.

"Calm down, Ling. You've been goading her this whole time. Don't be surprised she finally had enough of you."

Ling's eyes were wide and wild. He glared into Tommy's eyes, only inches from his own.

Tommy smiled. "We all get tired of you eventually, Ling," he joked.

It had the desired effect. Ling relaxed—just a bit, but enough to signal the fight was over. Tommy loosened his hold and Ling slid back onto his feet.

He pulled his clothes back into place. "Actually, I'm glad she finally stood up for herself," he said to Tommy as if I weren't even there. "Maybe you were right about her after all."

I didn't like the thought that they had been talking about me behind my back. I pushed myself to my feet. "Should we go now?" I suggested.

"Wait," said Rajiv. "Let me show you my totem."

I raised an eyebrow. "What for?"

Rajiv didn't seem to have an answer ready. Then he said, "If you are to join us, you should know our tools. In case you find yourself in a position to use them."

I still wasn't completely sure what these totems did. "What would I use them for?"

Rajiv smiled broadly. "When the time comes, you will know."

I shook my head at the predictably cryptic reply. Tommy smiled at me and gently patted my back. He left his hand there for a moment and it felt warm and strong. He took it away too soon.

"Go ahead and show us your totem," said Tommy. "Then we'll leave."

Rajiv stood up and we all followed him to a small cabinet in the corner of the room. He crouched down and undid the cabinet with a key he kept on a chain around his neck. But when he threw open the doors, his jaw dropped.

"It's gone!" he gasped.

Somehow I wasn't surprised.

FIFTY-FOUR54

"But, but, it's not possible!" Rajiv wailed. "It was here just this morning."

"That makes at least three totems," Tommy said. "Gabriela's, Ling's and now Rajiv's."

"Maybe four," hissed Ling as he jabbed a thumb at me, "if he got a hold of her brooch too."

"How many does he need?" I asked.

I thought it was a simple question, but Tommy looked at me like I'd just explained why Einstein was wrong about that whole $E=mc^2$ thing.

"What?" I shrugged at him.

He searched for words for a moment. "Until you asked that, I had assumed he wanted all of them. That we had more time. That as long as my bear was around my neck we were safe. But maybe he doesn't need all of them. Maybe he only needs some. Maybe it's already too late."

Ling stomped his foot. "Get a hold of yourself, Bluehorse! We still have time."

"How do you know?" I pressed him.

He looked at me sideways, not honoring me enough to turn his head to face me. "He is not trotting around the globe for fun. If he only needed three or four totems, he would have just ambushed us and taken what he wanted."

My brow creased as I considered the argument. Before I could consider it any further, though, Ling spoke again.

"Let's go. Maybe we can figure out where he will go next."

I looked to Tommy, but he just shrugged in agreement. So I joined in and shrugged at Rajiv. "Nice to meet you."

"It was a pleasure to meet you as well, Jeni. Good luck in your quest."

I nodded in thanks and we made our way outside.

"Now what?" Tommy asked.

Before Ling could answer, I stepped out in front of them and crossed my arms. "Now you tell me why you're lying to me."

FIFTY-FIVE55

Okay, it was bluff. I didn't really know they were lying to me, and I definitely didn't know about what. But I did know something wasn't right. Something about this Rajiv guy, and his missing totem, and Samara, and my mom, and just everything. So I decided to call them on it and see what they said.

Tommy didn't say anything. He narrowed his eyes and examined my face. Always careful.

But Ling immediately starting denying. That's how I knew I was right.

"Lying?!" he protested. "First you attack me and now you accuse us of lying? And after all we've done to help you find your mother."

That hit a nerve, but I knew that's what he was trying to do, so I ignored it, and him.

I turned to Tommy. "Well, Tommy Bluehorse?"

He paused a moment, then asked, "What do you think we've been lying about?"

Damn. That was the perfect way to handle it. He would be able to see what I suspected before he answered. But the problem was, I didn't know. The best I could do was try to turn it back on him.

"I think we both know. I just don't know why." He just smiled at me. Damn again.

I turned and walked to the street. "Let's go back to the hotel. I'm tired of this."

I raised my hand to hail a taxi. I couldn't see Tommy or Ling, and I figured they were gesturing at each other about me, but I resisted the urge to turn and look. In a minute, a taxi pulled up and we all piled in. It was a quiet ride, three people all lying to each other about something. When we got to the hotel, I jumped out and started toward the front steps, leaving Tommy and Ling to pay the driver.

Directly in front of the entrance was a circular driveway to drop off and pick up guests. Tommy ran up to me as I reached the door. Ling was still paying the driver.

"Jeni, wait!" Tommy took my hand. "I couldn't say anything with Ling standing right there, but—"

"Jeni! Jeni!" someone shouted.

I knew that voice. It was my mom!

I spun around only to see her being forced into a car in the driveway.

"Jeni! Don't be—"

But that's all she could say before they pulled her in and slammed the door shut. I ran toward the car, but it peeled out and sped away down the narrow Mumbai street.

Without hesitating I ran back over to the taxi and stopped it from pulling away.

"Follow that car!" I yelled and jumped in even as Tommy grabbed Ling and piled in the other side.

FIFTY-SIX56

The road was crowded with traffic and pedestrians, and the car with my mom in it had a head start. Despite the best efforts of the driver, it only took a few minutes until we knew we'd lost them.

"I am sorry, miss," the driver sighed at me. "I cannot see the car any more. I don't know which way it went."

I couldn't believe we'd been so close. I wasn't sure what to do. We weren't going to search Mumbai street by street.

Tommy leaned forward. "Where does this road lead to?" he asked the driver.

"The airport," was the answer. "It leads to the airport."

Tommy nodded. "That makes sense. They have the totem and now they can leave India."

Ling glared at me. "Now do you believe us?"

I ignored him. Instead, I tapped the driver on the shoulder. "Pull over when you can, please."

After a moment, the driver found a spot in front of some parked cars to pull over.

"What are we doing?" Tommy asked.

"We need to go to the airport and see if we can catch up with them," I answered.

"Agreed," said Tommy. "So why did we pull over?"

I shrugged. "All our stuff is still at the hotel."

Tommy squeezed his eyes shut. "Right. Okay. You guys go ahead to the airport. I'll go back for our stuff. Then I'll catch up."

I had hoped Ling would be the one to go back, but I didn't want to take the time to argue. Tommy hopped out and went in search of another taxi. Our driver pulled back into traffic and Ling and I headed to the airport.

"Well done," said Ling without really looking at me. "Now that's he's gone, I can tell you the truth."

FIFTY-SEVEN57

"The truth?" I turned to look at him. "What does that mean?"

"It means," he turned slowly and met my gaze, "that things are not as simple as you've been led to believe."

I thought for a moment. "My mother was the godling to the Japanese goddess of creation. I was supposed to become the godling on my fourteenth birthday, but my mom couldn't tell me because she was kidnapped by the godling to the Japanese god of destruction. Now I've traveled to three different continents in search of my mother so we can keep the bad guy from destroying the world. What's so simple about that?"

Ling looked away again, his mouth curling into the tiniest smile. But it was the first one I'd seen that seemed to exude actual warmth. "The actions have been complicated, but the basic premise is simple. And it isn't true."

"What's the basic premise?"

"That there are good guys and bad guys," Ling smiled, "and never the twain shall meet."

Ling looked back at me. "Not all of our traditions are as clear cut as that. Many cultures believed the gods of creation and destruction worked together. Some even believed they were the same god."

I didn't like what Ling was saying. "That doesn't really make sense."

"But it does," he replied. "We are in India. This is appropriate."

I waited for more, but apparently that was it. "Uh, why is that appropriate?"

"Because," Ling answered, "the godlings here are different from the rest of us. Hinduism is an ancient religion, but it is also a vibrant, modern one. It offers insight into some of the lost aspects of our own spirits."

I wasn't really getting his point. "Okay," I said anyway.

"Consider the Hindu god Shiva, for example," Ling went on. "A god of destruction, but also of creation. Do you see?"

I grimaced. "Yeah, I don't really know my Hindu gods so much."

Ling snickered. "Yes, that was ridiculously obvious."

I knew he'd just insulted me, but I wasn't exactly sure how. Before I could say anything, though, he jumped in again. "Let me try something you are more familiar with. Why did Noah build the ark?"

The question surprised me. "Come again?"

Ling smiled at hearing the expression again. "I asked you, why did Noah build the ark?"

Everyone knew that. "Because a flood was coming."

"What did the flood do?"

"It destroyed the world."

"And who sent the flood?"

"God."

"But who created the world?"

"God."

Ling's smile deepened a bit and he nodded. "Now do you see my point?"

I did. And it scared me. "Well, that's different—"

"No, it's not," he interrupted. "The only difference is that some people think in terms of us versus them, when really us and them are more alike than we want to believe."

I was about to reply, when he raised his hand. "Or more alike than we want others to believe."

I shook my head at that unexpected sentence. "What does that mean?"

"It means," Ling said looking down, his smile fading, "that some of us host spirits who are as destructive as they are creative. Some of us could easily be on the other side."

I thought I got it. "You?"

But I was wrong.

"No, not me," laughed Ling. "Tommy."

FIFTY-EIGHT58

Before I could say anything, the taxi came to an abrupt halt.

"We are here," announced the driver. "Chattrapathi Shivaji International Airport."

I was stunned for a second, wanting to continue my conversation with Ling, but faced by the protocol of exiting the cab now that we'd arrived. It didn't matter. Ling climbed out right away to pay the driver. I followed slowly, my mind racing with the implications of what he'd just said.

As we walked from the drive into the terminal, I asked him, "What are you trying to say?"

But it was back to the old, jerky Ling. "Hush! Not out here in public."

But the cab driver can listen? I thought.

I looked around. The terminal was packed with travelers. The world's second most populated city had an airport to match. I couldn't imagine we'd ever be able to see my mom in the throng of humanity packed into that hub. But maybe we didn't have to.

"We'll never find her in this crowd," Ling shrugged.

"Then let's find Nakajima instead," I said and headed toward the ticket counter I spied in the far corner. Japanese Airways.

It was just a hunch, maybe even an educated guess, but it was better than nothing. And somehow it felt right. It took a few minutes to force our way through the mass of people, but when we got close, I popped out of the crowd and bounced up to the sole ticketing agent, a young Indian woman with bright eyes.

"Can I help you, miss?" she asked with a smile, as Ling stepped up behind me, his clothes disheveled from the jostling journey.

"I'm looking for my uncle," I lied. I held my hand well over my head. "He's about this tall, gray hair, and um, Japanese."

The ticketing agent smiled. "Yes, of course. He was just here. Would you like me to page him?"

"No!" I replied a little too quickly and a little too loudly. "That is, um," I looked at Ling, "My boyfriend and I wanted to surprise him with a little going away present. We were going to surprise him here, but our taxi got caught in traffic."

"Boyfriend?" Ling whispered.

"Do you want me tell her the truth?" I hissed back.

He shrugged, then put his arm around me and smiled at the clerk. "We do love uncle Hiroshi."

I had to resist the urge to throw his arm off of me.

The clerk smiled again and nodded. "Yes, well. As I said he was just here. With a couple of traveling companions."

I wanted to ask if one of them was an American woman, but I didn't think I could do it calmly, so I bit my tongue.

The ticket lady looked down at her screen. "They're likely on their way to the gate now. Gate E54."

"E54," I repeated, hoping she would tell us where the flight was headed.

Instead, she simply confirmed, "Yes, E54."

So we thanked her and turned to find the nearest readerboard. Ling still had his arm around me so I pushed it off and headed into the crowd. He laughed—a cool, distressing chuckle— and we crushed through the crowd to the readerboard, which was still pretty far away. When we finally reached it we got two surprises.

The first was Tommy shoving his way up to us. "Hi. Just got here. Did you find them?"

But I didn't react because I was looking at the readerboard which said: 'Gate E54. Japanese Airways. Flight 1142. Cairo.'

FIFTY-NINE59

"Cairo?" I said. "What's in Cairo?"

Without hesitating, both Tommy and Ling gasped, "Massri."

I turned from the readerboard to look at them. "What's a massri?"

"Massri," Ling repeated. "Abdel Massri. The godling to the Egyptian god of destruction."

"Nakajima may be the oldest of them," Tommy said, "but Massri is the most powerful."

He turned to Ling. "Is Nakajima seeking permission?"

"I doubt it." Ling narrowed his eyes. "Massri wouldn't give it. More likely he's making sure Massri doesn't know what's going on."

That gave me an idea.

"What is it?" Tommy asked when I told them.

"I'll tell you on the way to Cairo," I replied. "Let's find out when the next flight leaves."

Then I took out my phone and a sent a quick text to Kyle. I didn't know if he'd get it, but I was going to need his help if this was going to work.

SIXTY60

We tried Air Egypt first, but it was sold out and already leaving the gate. So we went back to Japanese Airways.

"Did you find your uncle?" the ticketing agent asked me.

"Huh? Oh, uh no," I stammered. "That's why we need the next flight out."

Ling put his arm around me again. "She's cute when she's determined."

Tommy pulled Ling's arm away. "What are you doing?!"

The ticket girl stared at him, but Ling laughed. "Don't be jealous, Thomas. You had your chance."

Tommy stood there, speechless.

It was getting way too awkward way too fast.

"I'll explain later," I whispered to him.

"You better," he whispered back, then glared at Ling and his mocking smile.

The ticket lady was still staring at us all, but caught herself and quickly looked down at her screen. "Our next flight isn't until tomorrow. We only have one flight a day to Cairo. You might check with British Airlines, or Air Egypt. They have more flights."

I thanked her and we headed back into the crowd.

"What was that all about?" Tommy demanded once we were far enough away.

Ling laughed, and I just said, "I didn't know you cared, Mr. Bluehorse. I'm flattered. But we have business."

I glanced sideways at him and saw his cheeks burning red. I was more than a little glad that I could have that effect on him.

An hour later we were waiting to board British Airlines flight 3765 to Cairo. Six hours later we were landing. Seven hours later we were checking into the Pyramid Grand Hotel. And eight hours later we were in Tommy's room and I was ready to explain my plan. More than that, to start putting it into action.

"Okay, Jeni," Tommy sat on his bed. "What's the plan?"

I smiled. "Oh, you're gonna love this—"

But before I could say any more there was a pounding on the door.

"Open up! Open the door now!"

SIXTY-ONE61

"That's Kyle's voice!" I sprang up and pulled open the door. Kyle and Gabriela tumbled in and Kyle slammed the door behind them.

"You made it!" I gave him a hug. "You got my text?"

Kyle smiled. "Every letter of it."

I smiled back. "Good."

He grasped my hands and slipped the brooch back to me. His eyes told me he hadn't told Gabriela after all.

Then Gabriela cleared her throat. I'd forgotten how tall she was. I let go of Kyle and looked up at her. "Nice to see you too, Gabriela."

I don't think she believed me. She didn't answer. She didn't even smile.

I decided to change the subject. "Why were you pounding on the door like that?"

Kyle's eyes widened. "Someone was after us! As soon as we got off the plane. Right, Gabby?"

'Gabby?' I raised an eyebrow. They were getting awfully chummy.

"Yes, Kyle," she said. "I noticed them following us when we got off the plane. They even got into a second taxi and tried to follow us. I told the driver to lose them. I though he had, but—"

Kyle jumped in to finish. "But then we saw them following us on the street. We ran through some back alleys to get here, but I don't know if we lost them or not."

I looked at Tommy, who looked at Ling, who nodded.

"Massri," said Ling. "He knows we are here."

"Massri?!" Gabriela gasped. "How could he know already?"

I spun and pointed at Ling. "Because Ling is a traitor!"

SIXTY-TWO62

Tommy and Gabriela looked at each other wide-eyed. Ling sprang to his feet.

"How d— dare you?! How dare you call me a traitor!"

I couldn't help myself and started laughing. "Wow, Ling. Guilty conscience?"

"Wh— What's so funny?" Ling demanded.

"Yeah, Jen, what's the joke?" Kyle took a step toward Gabriela. "Is Ling really a traitor?"

"She's laughing at your reaction, Ling." Tommy stood up and gave Ling a pat on the back. "Relax. She's not your enemy."

I gave Ling a grin. "Although I did take you down in Mumbai."

I threw a glance at Kyle. "Capoeira."

He laughed. "Really?"

"Enough!" shouted Ling. "Why did you say I was a traitor?"

"That's the plan!" I threw my hands up. Why couldn't anyone figure out what I was saying? "We go to Massri and tell him that you're a traitor to the other godlings and I rejected the good Japanese god because I want the bad Japanese god. I want Massri to destroy Nakajima so I can have the bad Japanese god, and you want to help me because you're a traitor."

Ling's face froze in its angry countenance, then melted into that disconcerting grin. "That sounds ridiculous."

"It sounds dangerous," Kyle countered.

"It sounds perfect," said Tommy, clapping his hands. "Tell us the details, Jeni."

SIXTY-THREE63

The first part of the plan was finding Massri.

Unfortunately, even though Tommy and Ling and even Gabriela knew of him—knew all about him, it seemed—they didn't know where he lived, or even where he hung out or did his grocery shopping. So since we couldn't go to him, we needed him to come to us.

Or rather we needed him to have us taken to him.

He'd sent someone to follow Gabriela and Kyle. It was a good bet they were still looking for them, and maybe, probably, the rest of us. So an hour after I'd explained the plan, Tommy watched from across the street as Kyle, Ling, Gabriela and I sat in an outdoor café.

And badmouthed Abdel Massri

Loudly.

"Well, Massri is obviously a coward," I bellowed.

"Maybe he's just stupid," Kyle replied.

"He could be both," said Gabriela, almost yelling. "A stupid coward."

"And lazy," added Ling. "A stupid coward who's too lazy

and stupid and cowardly to show his face to us."

One thing was certain. People could hear us, and understand us. As it was pretty clear they knew who Massri was, and the implications of what we were saying. Everyone near us got up and either moved farther away, or just plain left the café. I started to worry the owner would kick us out before our plan had a chance to work. We'd been there for over an hour and the sun was beginning to set.

"Pardon me," came a raspy voice from behind me, on the other side of the short fence-like partition that separated the seating area from the road. The voice's owner placed a hand on my shoulder. It was cold and strong, gripping just tight enough to tell me it could grip a lot tighter.

I turned to face the man. He wore a fine black suit, with a black hat pulled down to shade his eyes. I guessed he was in his fifties, but it was hard to tell without seeing his eyes clearly.

"You should be careful what you say about Mr. Massri," he warned without releasing my shoulder. "He does not like being disrespected."

"That's because he's a big dumb j—" Kyle yelled before Gabriela put a hand over his mouth.

"I would like to apologize to Mr. Massri in person," I said. "Do you know him?"

The man smiled, exposing a few missing teeth in the front and a few gold ones in the back. "I know him. And he knows of you."

I nodded formally. "Will you take us to him?"

The man's smile thinned. "I will take you and you," he said pointing to me and Ling. Then he gestured toward Kyle and Gabriela. "But not them."

Kyle began to protest, but I stopped him. "That will be fine,"

I said. "I am the one who wants to speak to him."

"We know," the man rasped.

I raised an eyebrow. "How do you know that?"

The smile returned. "We know everything, Jeni Tanaka. More than even you know."

Then he turned and gestured for me and Ling to follow. We hopped the partition and hurried down the street.

I could hear Kyle telling Gabriela, "This is a bad idea."

I should have listened to him.

SIXTY-FOUR64

I had expected to meet Massri in some dark, marble chamber, him sitting bare-chested on a throne, torches flickering on the walls, maybe even some girls with palm fronds and a couple alligators in a pond.

It was actually pretty much the exact opposite.

He had an office on the top floor of a medium-sized office building on the outskirts of town. Even at dusk, it was bright from the large windows and cool from the central air. Massri met us in a conference room. The only other person there was the man who'd brought us. And there were no alligators to be seen.

He was in his early twenties, with pale skin and a shaved head. He wasn't bare-chested, but through his linen shirt you could see he had a powerful body.

"You could have chosen a more respectful way of getting my attention," was the first thing he said to us as we walked in. "I have a reputation among the locals here. I will now need to repair it somewhat."

"My apologies," I bowed slightly, although I wasn't exactly sure why. "We— that is, *I* wanted to see you. Our efforts to locate you were complicated by internal issues."

Massri raised his eyebrows at that, but he didn't immediately address it. Instead, he stood and gestured to the seats around the table. "Sit down. We shall talk."

I took the nearest seat, with my back to the door. Ling waited until I had selected my seat, then circled around to the other side and sat opposite me. It was obviously a deliberate choice. I figured it was some tactical maneuver and wondered whether Massri appraised it similarly.

"What sort of internal issues?" Massri asked once we were all seated. All except guide-man, who stood silently by the door.

"The others believe I am seeking Izamani no Mikoto, the Japanese goddess of creation," I said.

Massri folded his hands on the table top. "You are not?"

"No, I rejected her."

"I knew that," Massri said. "We all know that. Nakajima orchestrated that."

"You give Nakajima too much credit," I returned. "I rejected the goddess of creation because I want something better. Something more."

The corner of Massri's mouth curled into a tight smile. "And what is that?"

"Shinigami, the Japanese god of destruction," I answered.

Massri nodded thoughtfully, then looked at Ling. Ling gave only the slightest reply, a minimal nod, then looked at his hands. He was a terrible actor, I thought.

"That god already has a godling," Massri argued. "Nakajima himself."

"Which is why I have come to you," I said. "I have a proposal. A business proposal."

Massri spread his hands across his conference table and

looked around his office. I wasn't sure what kind of business he was in, but he was clearly successful at it.

"I like business proposals," he smiled. "What did you have in mind?"

Here we go, I thought. I looked at Ling for acknowledgement, or encouragement, or something. But he avoided my gaze. I figured he must be pretty scared. I had thought Ling was a better person for this than Tommy because, frankly, Ling was a jerk. I figured Massri was more likely to believe he really had gone turncoat. But right then, Ling was just sitting there, like he was waiting for it all to end. I hoped Massri would still buy the story.

"Ling and the others have been trying to help me stop Nakajima and rescue my mother," I explained. "They think when it's all over, I want to be the godling to Izamani. But what I really want is to rescue my mom, stop Nakajima, and take Shinigami from him. I wasn't sure how to make that happen until Ling told me he was willing to change sides and help the godlings of destruction."

"Now why would he do that?" Massri almost laughed.

Ling didn't look up from the table. He was doing a terrible job of selling it. I was really beginning to regret bringing him.

"Uh, because," I struggled, "because he's tired of the battle. And he realizes destruction and creation are two sides of the same coin."

Ling looked up at that. He offered a weak smile. "I did say that," was all he said.

"So what is your proposal?" Massri reminded me.

I nodded and leaned back confidently in my chair. The last bit of the sunset was swelling all pink and orange out Massri's western window. It filled the room with an apricot glow. "I help you stop Nakajima from taking all the gods' powers and you help me wrest Shinigami from Nakajima."

Massri nodded. "How can you help me stop Nakajima?"

I smiled and laid my hand on the table. "With this." I unfurled my hand to expose the chrysanthemum brooch, its green jewel gleaming.

Ling finally showed some life. "You *do* have it! You lied to me."

Wow, Ling, I thought. *Not really the time for this.*

"Not exactly," I said to him through a forced smile.

Then I turned back to Massri. "Nakajima thinks this is lost and is hoping to use my mother to coax Izamani back to a host—to him. When he starts the ritual, I pull this out and stop Izamani from entering him. Then you kill Nakajima and I take Shinigami instead of Izamani. You can have Izamani and any other godlings you can manage to extract through the ceremony."

Ling looked wildly from the brooch to Massri and back. Massri ignored him and pursed his lips in consideration. He reached toward the brooch. "May I see it?"

I could feel the deal closing. But I curled my hand back up. "Ah, ah, ah. Are you interested?"

Massri looked out the window as the last strands of sunlight disappeared in the faint clouds. "I like your plan, Jeni Tanaka. Wait for Nakajima to summon Izamani no Mikoto, then surprise him with your totem and steal both Izamani and Shinigami from him."

I smirked at Ling then looked up at Massri and unfurled my hand again. "So we have a deal?"

Massri stood up. "Oh no, of course not. I will implement your plan, but I shall do it myself."

Crap. I hadn't thought of that. "B— But you'll need me to get Izamani."

Massri smiled. "Do you know which god I am the godling to?"

"Uh..." I shrugged. "Tutankhamen?"

Massri's smile vanished. "He was a pharaoh, not a god," he spat. Then he regained his composure. "I am the godling to Apep, the serpent who one day will swallow the world."

I shrugged again. "Not getting it. Sorry."

He looked at the sun finishing its descent beneath the horizon then raised his hands toward me. From his shirt sleeves poured two black ribbons that spun in the air, then merged and transformed into a giant snake. It shot forward and wrapped itself around me even as I tried to stand up. I'd managed to get to my feet, but I was completely wrapped up by the snake, its coils constricting me into helpless immobility.

To say I was surprised would have been the wildest understatement. But it was nothing compared to what happened next.

SIXTY-FIVE65

I was about to yell, "Ling, help me!" but before I could, Massri said the words first. Only calmly.

I looked at him. "Ling, what's going on?"

Ling was smiling. He looked over at Massri, who smiled warmly back at him. Then Ling walked around the table to where I was suspended by the snake, my toes dangling above the floor.

"You were right about one thing," he said as he reached me. "I am a traitor."

Then he slapped me across the face. Hard. My cheek was on fire and I choked back a sob.

"That's for Mumbai," he hissed.

Then he wrenched the brooch from my hand.

"Goodbye, Jeni Tanaka," said Massri. "I will say hello to Izamani no Mikoto for you."

Then the snake tightened its coils and pulled its head away from me. The head grew to an enormous size and opened its gigantic mouth. Even as I screamed, "No!" it darted forward and swallowed me into complete darkness.

SIXTY-SIX66

At first, I thought I was dead. Then, I wished I were.

I awoke in a small room that could only really be described as a cell. My one connection to the rest of the world was a thin slit in the door at about the level of the top of my head. All I could see through it was the ceiling in the hallway.

I had no idea where I was or how long I had been there.

I just knew I was alone.

All alone.

Ling had betrayed me, and the others didn't even know where I was. How could they, when *I* didn't even know? And my phone was gone—they must have taken it—so I couldn't call or text anyone.

I didn't know what time it was. I didn't even know what day it was. I figured Massri or someone would come down to gloat at me, or feed me, or something. Then I began to panic as I realized they might not. They might just let me starve down here, then come get my body next week, or however long it takes someone to starve.

I pulled at the door and shouted down the hallway, but even as I did, I knew it wouldn't do any good. No one was coming.

I sat down on the middle of the floor and started crying. I didn't want to cry. I didn't want Ling to win. I didn't want Massri to win. I didn't want Nakajima to win.

I just wanted to go home. With my mom. That's all I ever really wanted. Just to get my mom back.

And maybe Izamani no Mikoto too.

I'd had a goddess inside me! But I rejected her because I was too stupid to know what was going on. I was being offered unimaginable power and I turned it down. I was being invited into the coolest clique on Earth, and I blew it. Spazzing out on the plastic deck while Chelsea Winters and the Gang ran away.

I wiped the tears away and scooted against the cold cement wall. I was tired. Too tired. I rested my head against the wall and wished it would all just end.

I might have fallen asleep. I wasn't really sure. Time had passed, but I didn't know how much. I wondered whether I'd dreamt the whole thing up, or was just crazy.

So when I first heard the voice, I thought I was hallucinating.

"Jeni?" came a whisper. A woman's voice. "Jeni?"

"Here," I whispered back. "I'm in here."

I pulled myself up and ran over to the door. I stuck my fingers through the slat above my head. "I'm right here!"

I heard footsteps come to my door, followed by the jingling of keys, and then the clunk of the door being unlocked. I darted outside to see Gabriela standing there, a ring of keys in her hands, and fear in her eyes.

"Gabriela!" I hugged her. "Thank you! You won't believe it. Ling is a traitor and—"

She shoved her hand over my mouth. "Silence," she commanded. "The door behind you leads to the outside. It is unlocked."

I turned and saw the door. I turned back to say something, but she stopped me.

"Go, Jeni," she implored. "I cannot help you any more. Go."

So I did. I didn't understand, but I decided I didn't need to. I ran to the door, pulled it open, then ran up the three flights of steps to the next set of metal doors. I pushed those open too and found myself outside, in the alley behind Massri's office building.

It was night. The serpent had swallowed the sun.

I ran as fast as I could back to the hotel.

I knew I wouldn't see Gabriela Paiz again.

SIXTY-SEVEN67

I probably should have worried about what I looked like running through the hotel lobby, but I didn't care. I sprinted past the front desk and up the stairs to Tommy's room. It was unlocked and I threw the door open.

But he was gone.

Really gone. Like, the room was already made up for the next guest. No Tommy, no suitcase, no cell phone. No nothing.

I darted down the hall to my room.

There was no one there either. But it wasn't completely empty. On the counter in front of the mirror was a note, with a British Airlines envelope underneath. I picked up the note and read it.

Jeni,

This is all just too much. I've gone home. You should too. There's a ticket to Seattle in the envelope. Use it to fly home. I'll see you there. We can let the godlings sort this out themselves.

Your Friend,

Kyle.

I sat down on the bed and looked at the airplane ticket. Even Kyle had quit on me.

SIXTY-EIGHT68

The front desk guy called me a cab and in no time I was at the airport. Without thinking—at least without thinking about what I was doing right then and instead thinking about everything else I'd done in the last few days—I walked zombie-like to the British Airlines ticketing counter.

So this was how it was going to end. Abandoned and betrayed by so called friends. Left alone to find my way home. Utterly failing to save my mother. Or regaining my godling birthright.

Even stupid Kyle abandoned me.

I stepped up to the counter, and looked up at the clerk without meeting her cheery gaze.

"What is your destination, miss?" she asked.

My eyes regained focus and I looked at her bright eyes. I started to reach for my ticket home. But I stopped.

"My destination?" I repeated.

"Yes," the clerk smiled even harder. "Where do you need to go?"

I considered how far I'd come with my so called friends. And how far I could go without them.

"Japan," I said. "I need to go to Japan."

SIXTY-NINE69

I arrived in Tokyo after dark and probably should have just found the nearest hotel. Instead, I took the last bus to the base of Mount Fuji. I didn't know a lot about ancient Japanese religious beliefs, but I knew mountains were sacred places, and Mt. Fuji was the greatest of the mountains. If Nakajima was in Japan, he was at Mt. Fuji, trying to steal the power of the creation gods and usher in an era of destruction.

I also knew that if Nakajima was there, so was Massri. And Ling. And maybe even Miguel Zapata, Samara Kapur, and the rest of the destruction godlings.

But none of that mattered because I knew my mom would be there too.

Unfortunately, I also knew who wouldn't be there: Kyle. Or Tommy. Or even Gabriela. It was just me against twelve evil godlings bent on world destruction.

There was a clearing up on a rise ahead of me. The entrance to it was marked by a massive wooden gate, its red and gold paint somehow managing to glimmer in what little light there was. I avoided the gate and crept up the side of the hill, my footsteps silent on the dewy grass. As I got closer I could hear voices. Not muffled voices. They weren't even whispering. Too cocky.

"Set up the altar, quickly." It was an older voice with a Japanese accent. Nakajima no doubt. "We've no time to waste."

"Why do you still need the American?" It was Massri. "We have the brooch."

"Insurance, my fine Egyptian friend," Nakajima replied. "I can't know exactly what Izamani will do. I need her to attempt to reenter the Tanaka woman, then I'll use the brooch to seize her away."

"Maybe I should just use it myself," Massri laughed, "like the girl said."

Then I heard a laugh I recognized. Ling's. I had to see the traitor. I didn't know what I was going to do, but I had to see what was going on. I crept to the top of the hill and peeked over, hoping I was far enough away to avoid detection.

Nakajima and Massri were at the center of the hill, lit by a single flashlight. Ling was near them, next to my mom who was bound at the wrists with a gag over her mouth. There were a few other figures milling about outside the glow of the flashlight, but I couldn't recognize them in the darkness.

I was pretty sure I was hidden in the darkness. Which is why I almost screamed when I heard Tommy whisper, "Jeni?"

SEVENTY70

He came out of nowhere, like the first time I met him, and crouched next to me on the wet grass.

"Jeni, what are you doing here?"

I was so glad to see him. But I was mad too. "I could ask you the same thing. You abandoned me in Cairo."

He didn't say anything, just stared at me with an expression I didn't fully understand.

"Ling's a traitor," I whispered. "He's working with Nakajima. Actually he's working with Massri against Nakajima."

He didn't react at all. Just a slight incline of the head. I thought it was an invitation to tell him more. Looking back, I guess it was, in a way.

I reached into my pocket and pulled out my mom's real brooch. The one I'd given Massri was the fake. I wasn't a complete idiot. Or so I thought.

"There's still time to stop them," I whispered. "This is the real brooch. The one Massri took was a fake Edo gave to me."

Tommy smiled at me. "Can I see it?"

He reached out and took the brooch from my hand. He

didn't say anything. Instead he just shook his head and stood up to slip the brooch into his own pocket. Then he looked down at me with those deep, soft eyes. They had that same sparkle I'd noticed when he'd jumped onto my back deck days earlier. That's why what he said next hurt so much.

"You still don't get it, do you? I— I really thought you were smarter than that. I really thought you'd figure it out."

I didn't understand. "Figure what out?"

"We never wanted you, Jeni. We just needed you close by."

Even in the cold night air, I could feel my face flush. "Wha— What do you mean?"

"That wraith in Rio? In Gabriela's apartment? That was Izamani no Mikoto. We barely kept her out of you." His voice split my heart. "We had to keep you moving, and in our sights, so we could stop it a third time if we had to."

My mind was racing. I couldn't think straight. "A third time?"

"We stopped it the very first time too," he went on. "We got your mom out of there before she could tell you what to expect."

"*You* did that?"

"Who do you think sent her the text?" Tommy answered. "I figured you found it on my phone and were just playing along after that. I guess not."

I couldn't believe what he was saying. I couldn't believe what was happening. I pulled myself up onto wobbling legs.

"I was just going to take you to Japan and keep you distracted while Hiroshi gathered the totems," Tommy kept talking, but I could hardly process what he was saying. "But when Zapata found you at the airport, we knew the creation godlings were trying to get to you. So we just kept you moving so they wouldn't catch up to you."

"We?" My head was spinning.

And he had the brooch. Damn him, he had my brooch!

"Me, Ling, Gabriela. Everyone you met. We're all destruction godlings. You'll never be one of them, Jeni. But you were never one of us either."

He grabbed a hold of my shoulders and kissed me on the forehead. "It's too bad. I kinda liked you."

He let go of one arm, but tightened his grip on the other. "Come on. Hiroshi will want to see you. And your brooch."

SEVENTY-ONE71

If I'd felt alone before, it was nothing to the feeling of utter betrayal and loneliness at that moment. Tommy was a destruction godling? The whole adventure had been a trick? I couldn't imagine feeling any more alone and loserish than I did at that moment. It was a million times worse than when Chelsea and the Gang walked out on me.

Which is why it was so sweet when Kyle came out of nowhere and flattened that bastard Tommy with a roundhouse kick.

"I brought the cavalry," Kyle smiled, and up the hillside marched Miguel Zapata, Samara, that girl from the plane. Even Not-Edo. And a few others I'd never met.

"Nice to meet you finally," said Miguel. "I am sorry you didn't know who I really was."

"I'm sorry too," I said. "I wouldn't have run away."

Gabriela was there too.

I pointed at her. "Kyle! Gabriela is one of them!"

"Not anymore," she answered. She took Kyle's hand. "I am with Kyle now."

Great. My supposed-to-be boyfriend turns out to be an evil, traitorous deceiver. But Kyle gets one of them to change sides.

I sighed. Good for Kyle. And me too, I realized. It explained why Gabriela had freed me.

"What are you waiting for?" Kyle asked me as I stood there, rooted to the spot.

"I don't belong here, Kyle," I said. "It was all a lie. Everyone abandoned me. No one was ever really my friend."

"I was," Kyle answered. "And I never abandoned you."

"What about the note you left me?" I demanded. "About quitting and going home?"

Kyle cocked his head. "My note said Tommy was a traitor and Gabriela and I had left for Mount Fuji because Nakajima was ready to perform the ritual."

I looked down at Tommy. He must have left me that fake note. I kicked his passed-out body.

"With Gabby's help," Kyle went on, "I contacted the other creation godlings. They were reluctant to embrace you since you'd rejected the goddess, but after we let them know everything you'd done, they agreed to help."

I smiled at him.

"But you're the one who has to end this," Kyle finished. "Show those godlings you're as good as any of them."

There wasn't time for any more pep talks. Kyle and the others' arrival had not gone unnoticed. Tommy was out cold, but the other destruction godlings, including Ling and Massri, had seen us. They all turned and headed for us, spreading out menacingly as they squared off against the creation godlings.

Kyle reached into Tommy's pocket and tossed me my mother's brooch. "We'll keep these guys busy. You stop Nakajima."

I caught the brooch and squeezed it tight. "Deal."

SEVENTY-TWO72

I ran toward the circle, and not a moment too soon. Nakajima had started whatever ceremony he had hatched and I could feel an electric chill in the air. He stood in the center of the hilltop, my mother on the ground next to him, and his hands raised to the sky. In one hand was an engraved dagger—his totem I guessed—and in the other was the fake brooch I'd passed to Massri. The fight at the edge of the hill was in full swing, shouts and blows filling the night air. Nakajima must have known he was short on time and this might be his only chance.

He was chanting—yelling really—into the sky, in some language I didn't understand. I supposed it was Japanese, but didn't really know. I didn't really care either. I just wanted to stop him from stealing Izamani's power. But I needed to hurry.

The night sky split open and the spirit I'd seen in Gabriela's apartment began descending down toward my mother—and Nakajima.

I ran into the circle and held the real brooch aloft. "Izamani no Mikoto! I accept you!"

The apparition paused in the sky above Nakajima, but only

for a moment. Then it poured out toward me and I closed my eyes, ready, finally, to accept my role as godling to Izamani no Mikoto.

I expected to feel the same electric shock sensation I had felt on my deck. And I might have gotten to, except that instead I felt the sensation of Nakajima tackling me. I smashed to the ground under his weight and the brooch flew out of my hand.

Nakajima jumped off of me and snatched the brooch off the ground. He held the brooch to his chest and all I could do was watch as Izamani poured through the brooch—and into him.

"Yes!" he shouted, his voice a chorus of three in one. "I did it. I command both Izamani and Shinigami! I will be unstoppable!"

And just in case no one was convinced, he began to glow and swell, rising into the night sky, seven, eight, nine feet tall.

"I will destroy all of you!" he boomed. "I will destroy everything!"

SEVENTY-THREE73

Nakajima continued to grow, even as everyone else started to run away down the hill. Well, almost every one. Kyle stayed. Gabriela stood at his side. Massri stayed too. But that coward Ling led the retreat of the destruction godlings.

I stood up and looked at Nakajima. What was happening to him reminded me of how I felt when Izamani entered me. It didn't work then either. If I could reject her, couldn't she reject Nakajima?

I ran toward him as fast as I could. He saw me coming, but was clumsy in his overgrown body and I executed a perfect leg sweep to drop his giant butt to the ground.

The hill shook as he hit, and his swollen head bounced on the ground with a thud. He dropped his dagger, but held onto the brooch. I snatched the knife off the ground, and jammed it into his wrist. His hand opened and I grabbed the brooch. I had expected blood to pour out, but instead it was light. Blinding rays of light shot out of the opening, his skin beginning to tear as the energy rushed out.

And I knew what to do. I finally knew what to do.

I turned and dug the knife into his shoulder and this time I twisted the blade. Light shot out of his shoulder even more intensely than from his wrist. Then I jumped over him so I could do it again and again on his other side too. When I'd finished, he had holes in his shoulders and arms and legs and hips, brilliant energy flowing and swirling from each opening up into the night sky.

I stepped away and covered my face. Nakajima let out a gargantuan yell, triple throated, then exploded in a burst of gold and silver light.

When I looked back I saw two spirits. One—Shinigami, I knew—scowled at me with dead, piercing eyes, then raced away, disappearing into the night.

But the other, Izamani no Mikoto, simply hovered above me, looking down at me.

"I accept you," I said.

And I accept you, I heard her voice in my mind.

She descended and surrounded me in a bath of light and joy, entering me to meld her spirit with mine. It was the same feeling of power and presence I had felt on my birthday, but this time I knew what it was, and I wasn't afraid. I was overjoyed. Izamani embraced me, and I her, a welcome guest. Then I opened my eyes to a whole new world.

Massri was the only destruction godling left. He looked at me, then laughed.

"Congratulations, Jeni Tanaka." He offered a facetious bow. "I am sure I shall see you again someday, but for now, here on your spirit's home ground, I cannot defeat you. So I bid you farewell."

With that, he slipped into the dark and disappeared.

I ran to my mother, pulled off her bindings and gave her the biggest hug I'd ever given anyone.

When we finally let go, I looked at her, tears running down my cheeks. "Izamani says hi."

She just smiled and hugged me again.

The other creation godlings came over to congratulate and welcome me. I finally belonged. It was a great feeling.

Then I saw Kyle.

He was standing on the far side of the hill. With Gabriela. They were holding hands and looking at each other, talking. Gabriela kissed him on the cheek. Then she pulled away and disappeared down the hill. Kyle watched after her for a moment, then wiped his eyes and sat on the wet grass.

I walked over to him, leaving my mom and the others behind.

When he saw me walking up, he rubbed at his eyes again and plastered a smile on his mouth.

"Looks like you finally found some friends who will accept you," he said gesturing toward the godlings.

I knelt down and hugged him, almost as long as I'd hugged my mom.

"No," I said. "I finally realized I always had that friend."

END

THE MAGGIE DEVEREAUX PARANORMAL MYSTERIES
Scottish Rite

Blood Rite

Last Rite

THE DAVID BRUNELLE LEGAL THRILLERS
Presumption of Innocence

Tribal Court

By Reason of Insanity

A Prosecutor for the Defense

Substantial Risk

Corpus Delicti

Accomplice Liability

A Lack of Motive

Missing Witness

Diminished Capacity

Devil's Plea Bargain

Homicide in Berlin

Premeditated Intent

Alibi Defense

THE TALON WINTER LEGAL THRILLERS
Winter's Law

Winter's Chance

Winter's Reason

Winter's Justice

Winter's Duty

Winter's Passion

ALSO BY STEPHEN PENNER
The Godling Club

Mars Station Alpha

ABOUT THE AUTHOR

Stephen Penner is an author, artist, and attorney from Seattle.

In addition to writing the Maggie Devereaux Paranormal Mysteries, he is also the author of the David Brunelle Legal Thriller Series, featuring Seattle homicide prosecutor David Brunelle; the Talon Winter Legal Thrillers, starring Tacoma criminal defense attorney Talon Winter; and several stand-alone works.

For more information, please visit *www.stephenpenner.com*.

www.ingramcontent.com/pod-product-compliance
Lightning Source LLC
Chambersburg PA
CBHW061228170626
46809CB00007B/2563